The White Aura

BOOK ONE
BY FELICIA TATUM

Felicia Tatum

Published by Felicia Tatum Books

PO Box 663

Monterey, TN 38574

www.feliciatatum.com

Cover by Whit and Ware

Editing by Rare Bird Editing

More books from Felicia Tatum:

The Vessel

Devlin's Descendant

Unbound Destinies

Mangled Hearts

Entangled Souls

Anxious Hearts

Bound Souls

Intoxicating Passion: The Box Set

Masked Encounters

Scornful Sadie

Sign up for my newsletter for a free download of
Entangled Souls!

Dedication

This book is dedicated to my wonderful daughter, Amelia. Everything I do is to make her life better. Mommy loves you, darling ☺

OLIVIA

My nails dug deep into the flesh on his back, and my lips found his soft, yet rough neck as my mouth filled with the salty taste of him. He growled and fisted my hair in his hands as he pulled my face to his mouth. I gently bit and kissed those magnificent lips, the tender skin plush under my teeth. A low rumble escaped his throat, echoing through my mind, as he pulled me closer. Soft lips kissed me harder and strong arms lifted me off the floor. My legs wrapped around his waist as he pushed me against the wall.

My gosh, he was a good kisser!

Gazing into those deep brown eyes, I lost myself in his soul. He was truly a beautiful boy, one I would never see myself being with in the waking world. I enjoyed our dreams together, as often as they were, and cherished each kiss, each touch, each look. He stirred a part of me I never knew existed, arousing me to want and need more out of my life.

Running my hands through his hair, I reached for him and pulled his lips back to mine.

BEEP! BEEP! BEEP! BEEP! I jumped out of the bed, catching my foot on the edge of the large yellow shag rug on my way to the dresser holding the alarm clock I hated so. Slamming the off button, I caught sight of my appearance in the mirror just long enough to wince and turn away quickly. My hair was wild, sticking out all over the place in tangled knots, while my tired face resembled a ghost or some other horrific supernatural being. Grabbing my brush, I hurried to the bed, not able to consider how crazy I looked in my just-waking state. The fierceness of my night was reflected in my hair, apparently.

The dream…I stopped brushing in mid-tangle to contemplate the vision from last night. The most recent of many, these occurrences were making me feel as if I had awakened from a deep slumber. Suddenly, my mind was sharp, and my body felt like a live wire. My mystery dream man was more real in my heart than I cared to admit, changing my state of being, the way my mind worked. Suddenly I daydreamed, doodled, and imagined the unknown.

I studied my slim, lanky frame that was beginning to get curves in all the places my parents were dreading. My breasts were getting perkier, my hips becoming rounder. Most seventeen year olds had more curves than me at this point, but my mother said, when she bothered to acknowledge me, I was a late bloomer in everything. Fantastic.

My deep red hair fell to my waist in tousled, loose waves. My bright green eyes sparkled like gemstones in the sunlight. *Red hair and green eyes. Really spectacular combination.* I couldn't have gotten seductive brown eyes, I had to get stuck with boring green. Nothing special to look at, that was for sure. My mother and father always told me I was beautiful, but isn't that what parents are supposed to think?

I ran the brush through my thick hair again, rearranging myself on the bed until I was cross-legged. For the last year, I had been having dreams about this guy who I had never met. The night of my sixteenth birthday, the sleep visions had begun, forever changing me. Did the two have a connection? I couldn't help but feel that the fluttering in the pit of my stomach was a sign that they did. I had started a journal that very morning, so I could remember everything, documenting the location specifics and what went on. The guy seemed to be about nineteen, if I had to guess, as he looked and acted only slightly older than me and my friends. He was tall, about 6 feet, with jet black hair and big brown eyes that looked like dark honey. He was totally gorgeous and I couldn't fight the feeling he was too handsome for plain Jane me.

Our locations varied. Sometimes we were in my room and sometimes a room that was decorated in dark colors and housed lots of books. Maybe it was his room, I didn't know. Occasionally we were outdoors in places I didn't recognize. The things we did also varied, but one thing was always the same: he never told me who he was. I had read a million books on dreams, and I still couldn't figure out why I saw the same guy every night. The dreams had no rhyme or reason, yet they felt familiar and safe. Like I was right where I was meant to be. Dreams are a part of our subconscious thoughts, according to all my reading, but why was he there?

Something surprising happened along the way. I felt as if I knew him, almost as though I'd fallen for my dream guy. As crazy as it seemed, I had this odd feeling he was somehow real. The turning and twisting of my gut told me to follow my instincts, and they led to him. When things weren't the right decision, I generally had a bad feeling, an intuition maybe, a sixth sense. I felt none of that with him.

There was something about the dreams that just felt...*strange.* Maybe it was the fact that the dreams were becoming somewhat sexual, but I was a virgin. Heck, I had only kissed one boy, and it was nothing like the kissing in these trysts. When I had kissed Brady, I hadn't felt much. It was pleasurable, but nothing like I'd imagined my first kiss would be. It was disappointing, like seeing the movie you kind of wanted to see instead of the one you had been dying to see. There were no sparks when our lips met like I'd always thought there would be. No fireworks going off while I was swept off my feet, dizzy with love and passion. Not like the dream kissing with my mysterious, sexy boy. Glancing over at the clock, I sighed, realizing I needed to get ready for school.

I walked to the closet and began rummaging through my clothing. I decided on a cute black skirt, ankle boots, a white shirt, and a scarf the same color as my eyes. I looked a little boring, but presentable. Fashion was something I always had been interested in, but I totally failed at really achieving the whole "cute girl" thing. Although I attempted to be unique, my outfits came out dull. Daring was basically a disaster no one wanted to even deal with, my attempts a combination of bad choice on top of another. I glanced at the clock as I heard my mother yell, "Olivia, it's time to go!"

Great, I was going to be late for school again if I didn't hurry. I threw my books in my white and yellow backpack and grabbed a cherry pastry from the kitchen on my way to mother's black SUV. She was seriously going to leave me one of these days. I had been begging my parents for my own vehicle for a year, but they wouldn't give in. Something about how I needed to figure it out financially and buy one on my own. If they would only help me, I wouldn't have to rush every morning to make sure I didn't walk to school in heels. My parents weren't like that, though. They rarely were around, paying me little attention, and I'd known when I asked that getting a car was a wish I wouldn't be granted.

The White Aura

"Heya, Momma! Sorrrrrrry. I couldn't decide what to wear," I said as I got in the car.

I always felt bad being late, but it was difficult to wake up and get going in the mornings after those crazy nights. My body tried to get ready for the day while my mind was stuck in the night before. I hadn't told anyone about them. Not that I didn't think my mom would be totally understanding—I had a feeling she would. It was just kind of weird being consumed with someone I'd never met, and telling my mom I kind of wanted to hump my dream dude was unthinkable. As I buckled, she simply stared ahead, nodding at my apology. If she was upset, I couldn't tell. My mother wasn't a very talkative person. She wasn't one of those moms who would butt in at every corner. If I had a problem, she listened and gave advice, but only if I went to her first. Otherwise, she observed from afar. While it was nice to a point, it also made me wonder if she actually cared sometimes.

In fact, I often wondered why my parents bothered with having children. My father wasn't much different than my mother, never giving advice. When I was growing up, they had always been there for the important stuff. Like plays, award ceremonies, and games. As the years passed, it seemed like they became more and more secretive. My brother, Kyle, who was twenty-eight, lived in another state. We'd never been close due to the large age difference and the fact that he only visited on holidays. Why was he so distant? Was there something about my family I didn't know? Did it play into why I felt them growing further from me? Were we in the witness protection program?

My mind drifted to my sexy dream man as some '70s song played on the radio and I watched the homes on the street pass by slowly. This guy was interfering with my thoughts. I wished I knew where he came from and why I was fantasizing about him. And why did it start on my birthday? The events had to be related. I tried to recall meeting him, but I felt only confusion. I would remember meeting him, wouldn't I?

"Olivia, dear, are you listening? We're almost to school," my mother was saying as I snapped back to reality.

"Oh, sorry, Mom. Just thinking about a test I have today." I lied yet again. It seemed to get easier the less they paid attention.

She nodded. "I hope you do well. How are you feeling today? Did you sleep well? Does anything hurt?"

Turning my head, I rolled my eyes. "I'm fine, Mom." She showed barely any interest in anything besides my health, which she was a little intrusive about lately.

We were turning in to the school parking lot, thankfully, and she cut her interrogation off. My mystery dream man would have to wait to invade my thoughts until later.

$\mathcal{SCOTT}$

I hated when she had to go to school. Or just wake up for that matter. Olivia Whitehead was the woman for me, my heart, my reason for breathing, for living, and she had absolutely no idea who I was. She made my heartbeat quicken at the mere thought of her beautiful face, but she didn't know me...not really, anyway. All she knew was the mystery man she loved to kiss in her dreams. Clenching my hand, I looked out the window, aimlessly watching a bird make a nest on the limb of a wide oak tree. If only it was time for me to meet her in her waking hours. It just couldn't occur yet. Too many bad things would happen if I found her before October 1st, exactly six months from yesterday, her seventeenth birthday.

I am a fifth generation sorcerer, which means I'm special to my family. Each firstborn in a generation is born with a different power they specialized in, but every five years, each family's firstborn sorcerer accumulates all the powers from the previous five years. For instance, one of my great-grandfathers, Philip Tabors, from the first generation, had the power to dream walk. That's how I went to see Olivia. When I relaxed my mind and body, my spirit would go to her. She thought she was simply dreaming, but our spirits were in fact visiting. All sorcerers can do magic, but the specialty powers are stronger and more complex for the firstborn sorcerers they belong to. My Grandma specialized in healing, meaning she could practically bring the dead back to life, and while my sister, Sadie, also had the ability, she wasn't quite as powerful in it because it wasn't her specialized power. She specialized in potions and charms, mixing and creating concoctions many others would be envious of. Every sorcerer specializes in specific areas of sorcery, but fifth generation sorcerers are the most powerful of them all.

When I was ten years old, all of my powers hit me. My awakening, the magical change, as the elders liked to call it. I remember it like it was yesterday. I woke up on my birthday, and as I stood, the power flowed through me, charging and bubbling my blood. My hand tingled as I lifted it in front of me and watched the glow of power as it consumed me. I was ten, so naturally, I attempted to blow stuff up and my father came flying in the room, chuckling when he saw the shattered dresser. "Your mother isn't going to be happy about that," he'd said, shaking his head as he waved his hand in front of it and pieced it all back together. It was the point I realized our whole family was special, and not just me.

We'd gone to my grandma's then, him antsy and excited like a kid eating cake. My mom and grandma waited on the porch, both glowing with excitement while my younger siblings played in the front yard. I watched them running around, wondering why we hadn't noticed any differences before. How could my family have been so magnificently different and I only now, thinking back, saw it? The mysterious way things appeared and disappeared, how Grandma always got to our house really quick, the way my parents always looked so much younger than my friend's parents. Everything was clear, like finally getting glasses after years of not seeing anything but blurs.

The White Aura

My father rushed me out of the car, and we'd all hugged and excitedly spoke before they told me everything. We went inside, where they all sat around me at the old oak table in the kitchen, looking at me like I had won the lottery, and explained who I was, what we did, how it worked. It'd taken years to learn the basics, but I was a quick study and excelled at our talents.

Ten years later, I had complete control of my powers, and I'd found the woman I was destined to be with.

She just didn't know this, and couldn't until October.

There was a curse on anyone in my family who fell in love. Apparently my first generation grandpa really pissed off another sorcerer, and since then, we've all had to pay. As sorcerers, we can sense the person we are supposed to be with the rest of our lives the moment we see them. Our heart mates, as we call them. But because of this curse, we couldn't let them fall in love with us "under any moon two quarters before their legal birthday." The first time I heard this, I laughed hysterically before realizing my parents were serious. It hadn't bothered me when I was a younger teen, cause really, who thinks about love then? I chased girls for the fun of it, but the moment I saw Livvie, everything changed. The complete and total feeling of consumption as my breath was taken from me was overwhelming, yet beautiful. I'd known nothing about her in those moments, but I did know I wanted no harm to ever come to her.

I found a loophole around the curse with one of my five specialized powers, dreamwalking. As a fifth generation, I had a lot of tricks up my sleeves, and I was more than willing to use any and all necessary. I could still see Olivia without breaking any rules. If the rule was broken, my love would die on her eighteenth birthday. So I had to be careful...very careful.

OLIVIA

"Liv. Liiiiiiiiv. Liv…."

I snapped my head up from my notebook covered in scribbly hearts. I had been doodling and hadn't heard a word my best friend had said. Standing just slightly shorter than me, Juniper had milk chocolatey skin and beautiful black curls that framed her face. Her hair wasn't so short she couldn't do anything with it, but not so long that she looked like the rest of the girls in our class. She had blue and light pink streaks dyed on each side, generally held back with some sort of headband or scarf. Today her big brown eyes were lined with heavy black liner while her hair was wild and free with a flower behind her ear. She loved music and always wore some sort of inverted quarter note; today's dangled from her ears. Our mothers met when they put us both in the same dance class at age three. We had been equally horrible at it, but that only solidified our friendship. Through the years, we'd failed at more sports than we'd succeeded, but we'd always done it together. Juniper was awesome and truly like a sister to me.

The White Aura

"I'm sorry, J. I was just doodling and didn't mean to ignore you." I grinned as I dropped the pen on top of the notebook. I didn't want to hurt my best friend by not giving her the attention she deserved. I'd been in my own little world lately, and I didn't want it to strain our friendship.

"It's ok! I was asking if you wanted to have a sleepover this week. I need an '80s dance movie marathon!" she squealed. She bounced in her seat, always full of energy. Footloose and Dirty Dancing were two of her favorite movies, and she insisted we watch them at least once a month.

Oh, how I loved my bestie. Her fun loving attitude and excitement were contagious.

"I'll ask my mom if we have anything going on," I said with a smile. Doubtful, considering my parents were away from home as much as possible.

The warning bell rang, signaling lunch was over, and we gathered our trash from the table. Juniper piled it on the tray while I stuffed my belongings in my backpack and slung it over my shoulder. We only had English and History left for the day. Yes, I'd lucked out and gotten a few classes with my best friend. It didn't happen often, as weird as that was for a small high school, but it was amazing when it did. I loved English but hated history. I just couldn't figure out why we had to learn about what a bunch of dead guys did. I knew they helped shape the country and everything, but did we really have to know every date and record of what they did? Was it necessary to *memorize* it all? I didn't think so.

I stood up and started to throw my leg over the bench when my arm crashed into something hard. I looked into Aiden Cavalier's eyes as he *oofed*. His dark gray, intense, and stormy eyes. He was the star basketball and soccer player for the school. Heck, he even ran track. Yeah, he was *that* guy. He was one year ahead of me, a senior, and the object of every female underclassman's affection. Except mine. I couldn't stand him. He was cocky and annoying with his "better-than-everyone-else-because-I-can-play-sports" attitude.

"Hey, Whitehead, what's the rush?" he said once he caught his breath.

I had an inkling he knew that I couldn't stand him. Perhaps that's why he talked to me so much. He was trying to win over the last holdout. I wished I'd hit him harder.

"Some of us don't get the privilege of being excused every time we're late for class," I said to him with a smile that was sweet but still said *I can't stand you*.

"Ouch. Jealous, are you, Whitehead? You could get the same privileges, you know. I've watched you run track. You're good. And you could hang with me...no one would bother caring if you're late." His overly-confident attitude destroyed all good looks he possessed. His brows did that awkward thing boys do when they look a girl over as he stood there ogling me.

Oh, my gosh. I seriously wanted to slap the smirk off his face.

"I actually don't like being late for class, *Cavalier*. I like keeping my grades up, and I want to get into a good college based on my brain, not my physical abilities," I snapped at him. How did he annoy me so quickly and with so few words?

I walked away and got as far as the cafeteria doors when I realized he was beside me. I rolled my eyes and kept on, speeding my pace a bit as I wondered where in the world Juniper had run off to. She had gotten up two seconds before me and escaped this awful interaction. The bell rang again, and I found my opportunity to lose Aiden, thank goodness. I sped up when students poured out of a classroom, and ditched him in the crowded hall.

I got to my locker just as J arrived, her eyes gleaming with mischief and dancing in excitement.

"Where were you? I needed backup!" I said, exasperated.

"Sorry, sorry. I know you can't stand—"she nodded her head in Aiden's direction,"but he's adorable and I think you should give him a chance. I'm pretty sure he likes you, Liv." Her sneaky grin made me roll my eyes for the second time in less than five minutes.

Oh, brother. Was she serious? Leave it to Juniper to be all love-struck on a guy based solely on looks. She was always on some hot guy kick, swearing I was too pretty to be single, and I needed to date someone already. I loved her, really, but she was annoying with the boy obsession. It was partly why I was hadn't told her of my dream man. She would take the information and go crazy with it. Figuring out what was going on was difficult enough without my best friend planning a wedding, or some other ridiculous event, because she found out.

I snagged my English book and started walking to class, glancing around to avoid any other unwanted encounters. This was the only one J and I didn't have together this year. She got the good teacher while I was stuck with the worst in the grade, the one who gave all the homework and the hardest tests. Focusing was a must because I absolutely could not fail, so I would have to wait until history to scold her about the Aiden nonsense. *Aiden Cavalier liked me? I didn't think so. Me give Aiden a chance? Absolutely deplorable to think of either.*

SCOTT

The coffee shop on 4th Street held memories from the day I first saw my love walking down the street. Dressed in casual clothing with a light scarf wrapped around her neck, hair flowing, she'd literally taken my breath away. She'd walked quickly, eyes cast straight ahead. There was this overwhelming feeling in my gut, a tingly sensation setting me on fire when she neared, and I'd jerked my head up as the emotions took hold. I knew she was to be my heart mate for all eternity based on the stories I'd heard from my parents and basically every sorcerer who'd found their other half. I'd rushed to the door, stepping outside to see her disappear around the corner. From that moment forward, my heart was lost to her. My thoughts were consumed with her silky red hair, and my eyes longed to peer into hers. The protectiveness I felt for her was overwhelming. I would do anything it took to keep her safe.

Following her, not my proudest moment, I'd caught her meeting up with someone and heard her name. Olivia. It echoed through my mind, singing to my soul. After some stealthy stalking, all in the name of love, I'd heard her last name. Though familiar, it didn't ring any immediate bells, but gave me enough to locate her in my dreams. Her face alone would do it, but a name made it so much easier. From there, I'd begun my dreamwalking.

As sorcerers, we stopped aging at age 25. We looked 25 for a thousand years and then began to age at a very slow rate. My grandmother was at least 1500 and looked no more than 50. I was not sure of the exact number because she's very sensitive about her age. Learned my lesson the hard way when I'd discovered our sorcerer trick with our aging.

It was sorcerer law that we absolutely could not do a spell to make a human stop aging. Unless....the human was yours. There was a whole process the council would go through to prove you were indeed linked with the human. Once they determined a positive heart link, the spell was cast. This was set into place so we could be with our heart mates for life. The council mostly regulated and enforced, but occasionally something big would happen between supernatural beings and they would have to intervene. So far, I hadn't encountered them, and hoped I wouldn't until Livvie and I met, and then I would have to.

I snapped back to reality as my grandmother swayed into the room, using her magic to throw the door open with the swish of her hand. She was sometimes dramatic with her powers.

"Hey little one, is something troubling you?"

She called me little one, even though I stood at least a foot taller. It began when I was small, following her around and asking a ton of questions when I'd visit. As I grew, the name embarrassed me a few times, but then I started to not care. And of course, she didn't care about my height and only smirked and shook her head when I pointed it out.

"No, Grandma, just thinking of the first time I saw Livvie. I wish I could see her in the waking hours...this dream stuff isn't enough for me," I said sadly. I was closest to my grandmother. She didn't want to shield me from my powers as much as my parents did. I could be just me when around her. I'd rushed to tell her all about Olivia the day I saw her and felt our connection.

"Little one, you know that you have to wait, or she will die. This curse is evil and I wish we could change things." She paused like there was something she wasn't sure she should say. "There is a legend stating that if you kill the descendant of the sorcerer who cast the curse, the curse is broken forever."

"What? Why hasn't anyone told me about this before?" I almost screamed at her, interrupting her sentence. I snapped my head up, my eyes wide. The shock of her words made me quiver in anger and hope. What if I could prevent anyone else from ever having the worries I do now? Could I save the family while also securing Olivia's safety?

"Little one...it is legend. If it were true, it would more than likely start a war. It would be murder. It's not worth it. You can wait six months; it will be painful, but you do have the advantage of dreamwalking. Others before you haven't," she said with her voice soft. Warmth flowed through me and my heartbeat calmed. She'd been around much longer than I and had probably seen many of our ancestors suffer from not being with the one they love.

She was right. I loved my grandma, and I admired her because she was so wise and knew me so well. She stood barely five feet tall, with dark brown hair that was beginning to get gray strands here and there. She had eyes the color of the ocean. Because she was a healer, she had a soothing air about her that was a comfort to any living creature in her presence. One look at her and no one would believe she was one of the most powerful sorceresses on the planet. Tiny, compact, and full of magical energy that could knock anyone into tomorrow.

I had heard many stories about her, and many legends were in our books about her fights in the 1800's. It was amazing, the things she had survived. She had defeated many grotesque creatures and destroyed some very powerful sorcerers. She had even fought vampires and won, something unheard of in our community. Vampires normally weren't as civilized as sorcerers, many of them going rogue and using their abilities to deceive and destroy. Some were good, but most weren't. Vampires were sneaky and almost impossible to kill, using their charm and strength to outwit and conquer. Yet Grandma had killed quite a few in her day. She was my hero.

"Why don't you just listen in on her for a little while? You'll feel connected with her and maybe it won't be so painful," she suggested with a smile and turned to leave. Once a sorcerer linked with his or her human, it became very painful to be away. We became ill and slowly began to die without our heart mates. It seemed all in my family knew of their heart mate before age eighteen, so we had all had our share of pain. Luckily no one had died yet, but a few had come very, very close. Damned if I let my Livvie be the first. Grandma had a magical concoction to lessen the pain, and though our heart mate tie was new, I would have to begin mixing and drinking it to survive. Our spirit encounters didn't have the same effect as a face-to-face meeting, but it definitely helped.

Slowing my breath, I relaxed and focused on stilling my anxiousness. Dreamwalking and espying took a lot of power and concentration, which wasn't the easiest when I consistently thought about the worst outcome possible, but somehow, I managed to push those bad things from my head and let being in her presence consume me. Leaning back, I rested my head on the chair and closed my eyes, willing my spirit to find hers, to connect.

OLIVIA

History was my last class of the day, and I was beyond ready to head home. Mr. Mayfield, my English teacher, had been in an awful mood. Our reflection papers hadn't been the best, and he spent most of the class chewing us out for it. I really shouldn't have been concerned, because I made a 93, but something about being yelled at as a group irked me. I understood the majority needed the extra lessons, but it annoyed me nonetheless. Sending me to the hall or letting me sit and read could have been a better use of my time.

So then in History with J, I couldn't concentrate. We had less than a half-hour left. Currently, Mrs. Steele was going over the Cold War, her voice lulling me to sleep as she droned on straight from the textbook. I knew that all of this information would be on the next test, but I couldn't make my mind pay attention. The kid behind me was clicking her pen in and out, over and over. That noise drove me crazy, and it took all I had to not yank it out of her hand and throw it across the room.

"Psst."

I looked to my left, seeing Juniper hissing out the side of her mouth and sliding a note across the floor. Lifting my foot, I stopped it from going under my desk. With a nonchalant fake yawn, I dropped my pen and picked up the note.

"So what's up with u and Aiden? –J"

I just shook my head at her. No way would I have this conversation in class. Especially through a note. Her face fell, and I could see the disappointment, but I couldn't let that get to me. Juniper was my best friend, so I knew she meant well, but I couldn't tell her that a tiny part of me was actually attracted to Aiden. She was very outgoing, and the minute I let it out, she would do everything she could to "help" me with him and end up embarrassing me. The whole school would think I wanted to date him, his ego would inflate and probably explode, killing us all. It really was a dangerous situation to tell J anything about boys.

Besides, I didn't know if I wanted to date him or anything. But I did like the attention that the hot senior in school was giving me. It didn't exactly hurt that he had dreamy eyes that seemed to be able to see inside my soul, and I often found them turned in my direction. All girls dreamed of this, didn't they? Being the center of some boy's attention? A popular boy's attention that everyone else happened to want...it was the stuff movies were made of.

What was wrong with me, though? By night I'm dreaming of this hot guy and totally almost sexing him up. By day I'm acting like I couldn't stand the school jock and secretly wanting him to pay a little more attention to me. Did I want either one of them? Heck, was the sexy guy even real? If my dream man were real, I wouldn't think twice about Aiden, but I couldn't live my life relying on dreams to make me happy. I didn't know. Maybe he was someone I had seen in passing and now he had taken over my nights. Or maybe he was an actor I saw in a movie so bad that I tried to rid myself of the memory of watching it but remembered him.

Either way, the obsession was insane.

The bell rang, startling me from my thoughts. I looked around and saw the class furiously scribbling something down on their papers. Oh, well, I'd have to ask Juniper about that later. I gathered my belongings and hurried to my locker. Juniper wasn't far behind me. I knew what she was going to ask, though, so I threw my History books in, grabbed my math folder with homework, and turned to go.

"Olivia!"

"Hey, Whitehead."

Juniper called from behind me and Aiden from my right, but I ignored both. I wasn't in the mood to listen to either, so I just kept walking, dodging in and out of the crowd of students until I made it out the back door. Neither of them would find me this way. I walked the back way to track practice, not looking behind me once.

My feet pounded the track as sweat dripped from my forehead and slid down my face. My heart pounded, and my breath came fast. Running was my escape. Practice was finished twenty minutes ago, but the frustrations from everything weren't gone. So I ran. The sun was setting, but not enough that it was dark, yet. The orange-yellow sky gave a calming backdrop as I worked out my feelings.

I completed a circuit of the track when I heard a whistle. I slowed, breathing deeply to calm my insides, and saw Aiden standing by the bleachers. I looped around and came to a stop beside him. I worked to catch my breath as I stretched my body. Running was exhausting. "Hey," I said in between breaths.

He gave me a half smile. The wind gusted lightly, causing his hair to ruffle. His eyes were bright and mysterious. As always. "Heya, Whitehead."

Seeing him standing in the dimming light made my heart beat faster. He looked at me intently, and I couldn't stop myself from wondering how long he had watched me. "What are you doing here?"

"I wanted to talk to you after practice, but you kept running. So, I waited."

"The whole time?"

"Yep." He looked around briefly, reached into his back pocket, and produced an ice cold water bottle. He half bowed and presented it to me like he was a butler.

Laughing, I took the water. "Thank you oh-so-much, kind sir."

"No problem. Hey, I'm here for you, Whitehead. At your service." He flashed that fabulous smile, and I couldn't help but smile back. He moved closer.

I looked up at him and noticed him staring. I took a long drink. The cool liquid felt amazing sliding down my throat, and it helped me to stop thinking about Aiden's eyes. "Wanna walk for a few minutes? Just once around the track..." I needed to cool down.

"Sure. I'd love to spend more time with you."

We kept a steady pace. We were both runners, so walking wouldn't tire us out easily. I sipped more water and wondered why he wasn't speaking. "What did you want to talk to me about?"

"I just wanted to hang out. I want you to like me, Whitehead. What better way than to let you get to know my amazingly fantastic personality?" he asked while bumping his body into mine.

My skin felt alive after the explosive contact with his. As much as I didn't want to be, I was attracted to Aiden Cavalier. "Then tell me more, Cavalier."

"I'm not as smart as people think I am. I'm just good at memorizing the information. If you asked me half the stuff on my History test, I couldn't answer it now," He leaned in like he was letting me in on a big secret. "And the test was this morning."

I laughed loudly and punched his arm. "People don't like you for your brains. You're mister jock star. Remember?"

His face fell a little. "Oh, yeah. I'd rather people think I'm smart. Being a jock isn't all it's cracked up to be. Yeah, I get privileges...I have a good body...teachers think I'm a god...which is all fine and dandy. But then...I meet someone like you. You aren't impressed by any of that, are you?"

He looked sad, and I couldn't help reaching to comfort him. Seeing someone hurting pained my heart and I couldn't stop myself. I placed my hand on his arm and squeezed him. "No. I'm not. Realizing that is kind of impressive, though." I winked at him.

His eyes got wider, and his face lit up. He hugged me, and I felt the warmth of his body pressed against mine. I breathed in his scent and felt dizzy from it. I leaned back and looked into his eyes, and they looked like he wanted to kiss me. I pushed myself away and said, "Well, thanks for waiting for me, Aiden. This walk was fun, but we've circled around once.

I really need to get home and cleaned up." I turned to walk, grabbing my towel and the empty water jug I drank at practice.

He started to talk, but I rushed off. My legs screamed at me to slow, but I couldn't. Pushing forward, I hurried to the locker room, only relaxing once inside. I felt bad about leaving so abruptly, but I had to get away. Being that close to Aiden...smelling him and holding him...it was dangerous. If I didn't want to end up wanting him, I must be more careful.

SCOTT

Time was slipping away, my mind focused on Olivia instead of school, and I was going to be late for my English class. Less than five minutes to get to my building, and I was on the other side of campus. While I could use magic to get there, it was a big risk of exposing magic to society. I'd rather be late. My feet pounded through the grass covering the last courtyard, my backpack beating me up along the way. Out of breath, I stumbled up the stairs and in the front, running smack dab into a crowd of students. "Excuse me. I'm sorry." I yelled my apologies as I hurried up the three flights of stairs to my classroom. I looked at my watch, seeing I only had one minute until class began. My professor was the type who locked the door precisely at starting time. I couldn't afford to miss another class, especially this close to finals.

My major was still undecided, but I knew I wanted to work with art; whether creating it, teaching it, or selling it. Picking a definitive career path wasn't the easiest decision I would make, but I continued to remind myself I could always go back to school to try again if I didn't like it. I wouldn't age for a while, so it wouldn't be like the other students would know and create an awkward situation. Snorting as I finished the last of the stairs, I thought to how cool it would be to look so young while being so much older and wiser. Not to mention the magical abilities.

Skidding to a halt at room 325, I flung the door open, hitting someone on the other side. Abashed, I slowly dropped my hand from the knob and looked around the door, right into the stern face of my not-so-amused professor. My mouth dropped open and I muttered an apology. Horrified by almost knocking my professor out, I rushed to my seat. Grabbing my notebook, I attempted to be as quiet as possible. It didn't really work because I accidentally dropped my backpack on the floor. Professor Galloway gave me a look designed to stop my heart: brows creased, eyes slit narrowly, and mouth pursed tightly. I lifted my hand in an apology.

He was an older man, his skin aged and wrinkled, hair white and thinning. He wasn't the largest of men, but his presence filled the room and he held himself in such a manner that everyone listened when he spoke. His voice was loud and demanding, not matching his outer appearance in the slightest. Each word boomed from his mouth, causing the class to sit tall and focus on him. No one dared use their phones in his class. Only one student was brave enough to bring a computer, the rest of us handwriting our notes. As terrifying as he was, I respected Dr. Galloway.

Nonetheless, I found myself drifting off, spending the rest of the class lost in thoughts about Livvie. How was I going to survive the next five months and some odd days? I longed to be able to talk to her, to hold her in real life, and to just enjoy her company. Our dreamwalking didn't allow me to get to know her as much as I desired. I wanted to know everything there was to know about her. Her favorite places, her favorite foods, her favorite subject in school. Everything. Visiting her in dreams wouldn't help me accomplish that. In fact, I wasn't sure she even believed I was real.

The White Aura

How could I convince her? Living in pure torture for the coming months wouldn't do. My heart was fragile as it was, and if Livvie didn't believe, didn't know my love was true and something she could have for eternity...well, I couldn't imagine what I would do. Not only must I keep my distance and manage to survive, but now I must find a way to prove to her I am more than a part of her dream world. Prove I would be a part of her waking world in a few months.

The shuffling of book bags and people moving broke my trance. Glancing down at my wrist, I saw class ran over and I'd missed most of it. Stuffing my blank notebook back in my bag, I moved my way to the front of the class, stopping to apologize to Professor Galloway one last time. This would probably affect my grade in the long run. As long as I passed, I guessed it didn't really matter.

OLIVIA

Lying on my stomach on my bed, I flipped through the songs on my mp3 player. I was frustrated that I couldn't find one to fit my mood. Not that I knew what my mood was. I was upset with Juniper for implying Aiden was showing interest in me, though I wasn't quite sure why that made me upset…perhaps because deep down I knew it to be true. I was also annoyed with my parents for working too much. Most of all, the most important factor of my mood, was the fact that I was dreaming about some strange person and I couldn't stop thinking about him. I mean, who does that?

The phone rang and J's picture popped up on the screen. Sliding the screen, I answered.

"Hey, J."

"Hey, Liv, are you still upset with me? I was calling after you while you were at your locker."

I knew that sound. It was caution and sadness mixed together. I picked lint off of my skirt.

"No, J, I'm not mad. I dunno what's up with me today. I didn't hear you," I lied. "Hey, why did you say that stuff about Aiden? He doesn't like me," I said it so sharply that it sounded angry. What if Aiden did like me? What could I do about it? I couldn't stand the guy most days, but the thought of hurting him upset me. A lot. Connections were a weird thing, happening randomly and without warning, and for some reason, I thought I had one with Aiden.

"Wellllllllll….." she started with her I-know-something-you-don't-know-but-will-want-to voice.

Oh, fantastic.

"He asked me for your number today after school. And I gave it to him."

"You did what? Without asking me first?" I asked in shock. Jumping to my feet, I paced the floor. And even kicked the wall, which bruised my toe. Why would he ask her? He waited for me after practice and didn't say anything about it. "I can't believe you did that!" Trust was something I thought I had with Juniper, but this was making me wonder.

"Liv…I think you're just scared, but I'm going to help you…" She was cut off by a beep. Call waiting. A number I didn't know. Hmm, wonder who that could be.

"Gotta go, J. My mom is calling." I hung up before she could protest.

"Hello," I said timidly.

A deep voice answered, "Hello, is this Olivia?"

Oh, dear.

"Yes, it is. May I ask who is speaking?"

"This is Aiden. I hope you don't mind, but I asked that music girl you hang around with for your number."

"Music girl?" He didn't even know her name. "She's called Juniper, and I guess it's ok...though, I'm not sure why you didn't just ask me after practice today." I hoped he would tell me why he wanted to talk.

"Yeah, sorry about that. I don't know what I was thinking. Sooo...uhh...I was wondering if you...listen, I know you don't like me very much, and that's weird to me, because all of the girls like me, but I was wondering if you wanted to go to the spring formal with me?"

It all came out in a very fast breath. Was he nervous?

"Umm...well, you're right. I don't like you very much. You're cocky and arrogant, in my opinion."

I couldn't be anything but blunt, no matter how hard I tried. I had been a difficult child to raise, or so I had been told. My parents had great stories of my abrupt manner at some of our holiday parties. He laughed a deeply and I realized he didn't sound so bad on the phone.

"Well, I want a chance to change your opinion. Will you let me try?" His deep voice rumbled through the earpiece, and my heart jumped.

I did need a date to the formal...and I would take any excuse to buy a new dress.

"Ok, Cavalier, I'll consider giving you a chance, but if you do something between now and then to totally turn me off, our deal is off," I spat. "And this isn't a yes, this is a consideration." I quickly hung up the phone. What was going on with me? I was some kind of crazy lady lately.

The White Aura

Aiden had transferred to our school when I was a freshman and had immediately attracted everyone's attention. The girls all wanted him, the boys all wanted to be him. He had always seemed full of himself though, using his athletic standing to his advantage in every way he could think of: missing tests, skipping classes, sometimes even skipping school. It was ridiculous. I kind of thought that maybe he had a hard home life, because no one ever showed up for him at games and ceremonies we held. He also never spoke of any siblings, so it was like he didn't have anyone. I almost pitied him. When my parents weren't around, I at least had Juniper to talk to. He didn't seem close to anyone like that. I threw the phone on the nightstand and flung an arm over my eyes. Then I heard the front door open, so I got off of bed to greet my mother.

"Hey, Mom."

"Hey, baby girl. How was your day?" She reached out to hug me, a rare thing these days.

I led her to the kitchen table, and I told her about everything that happened. From the sleepover request to the odd interactions with Aiden. She listened intently, and when I finished, asked me a question that floored me.

"Are you sure you aren't interested in this boy, Olivia?"

I just stared at her. Maybe she wasn't listening intently after all.

"Mom…I just said he's in love with himself and snobby. Why would I like him?"

"Well…you did just say yes to the spring formal…doesn't sound like you're entirely disgusted by him. Just an observation."

She winked and stood up to start making dinner. Pots hit the counters with thumps, and silverware sliced the vegetables on the cutting tray. Oh, my gosh, everyone in my life was mental today. I stood and walked to the island in the middle of our kitchen. I chopped onions for our sauce, deciding I would just ignore her comments for now.

"How was work?" I asked.

"Fine," she stated, turning from me to stir something bubbling in the pot.

"Did anything happen?" Asking questions about her job were difficult since she rarely told me anything about what she did, and never told me about who she worked with.

She shook her head, still facing away. "No."

Talking to her was like trying to pull teeth. I sighed, not knowing what else to say and leaving it at that.

"How is Juniper?" she questioned.

"Fine," I replied, hoping a dose of her own medicine would make her realize how truly annoying her attitude was.

"Is the sleepover here or at her house?" she asked, finally giving me a glance.

"Her house, I think," I responded. We took turns, often spending every weekend together in one way or another. "We were here last weekend."

She nodded. "Be careful, Olivia. There are bad people in this world and I worry about you," she said, brushing my hair from my face.

Her words were simple, but there was such worry behind them it caused me to think twice. What was going on? Were my parents in the mafia or something? Why would she warn me like that? "Umm...ok."

She snapped back to herself, distancing us and refocusing on the meal. "Will you set the table, please? Only two, your father won't be in until late."

"Oh? Where is he?" I quizzed.

"Working," she responded curtly.

And that was the end of any mother daughter bonding we may have stumbled into. Why my parents were so obscure, I couldn't tell you, but it sucked. Would I ever feel like they cared?

SCOTT

"Dammit!!!" I threw a book across the room. Pacing with my hands in my hair, I tried my best to not punch the wall. I had plugged in just as Livvie and her friend had started talking. I couldn't hear the other end of the conversation, but I noticed she was frustrated. Then she talked to someone else, and I knew it wasn't her mother like she told her friend, because she seemed nervous, and the conversation wasn't the kind you have with someone like a parent. She spoke to the person on the other line about proving himself. At least, I suspected it was a male, and Olivia confirmed my suspicions when her mother actually came home. She had a date. For the dance. The one I absolutely couldn't take her to because it was in two weeks.

Picking up the book, I stuffed it in my backpack. I went back to campus because I'd forgotten to turn in a project to my art professor. The quietness convinced me to stay and study.

I was in my second year of college and needed to pick a major soon. Painting was my passion, but I wanted to major in something financially acceptable. I needed to start putting away money. After all, I had a very long life ahead of me. More than one degree was certainly an option, but what to do first was the question.

I found this little nook on the top floor of the library one day last week when I was looking for some reference materials. I noticed the open door, away from the books and computers, and stuck my head in to have a look. The small room contained a comfy chair and a long table. I assumed it was meant for studying, but I never saw anyone else using it.

It was perfect for when I needed some quiet time to study or to check on Livvie. When I espied, I looked like I was simply resting my eyes, but if someone tried to talk to me, I couldn't respond. For this reason, it was best if I did it someplace with little or no human traffic.

I glanced around to make sure everything was as when I arrived, then headed home.

After turning on every light in the apartment, I sat on my bed. Resting my head in my hands, I just stared at the floor. I had no idea what to do. Going to her was out of the question. I couldn't physically meet and make her fall for me. Not yet, anyway. I blindly looked around the room when a book caught my eye. Not the large, torn black text I threw, but another. One of the accounts of my family's history. Was telling her the truth an option?

Loopholes were tricky things, and with her life on the line, I walked a slippery slope. I didn't want to do anything that could cause the curse to be activated even sooner. I strode across the room, lifting the brown, leather-bound volume from the shelf. It was wide and heavy, the binding torn and worn down. The pages were yellow and weathered by age, which was expected. It had been in the Tabors family for many years.

Opening the cover, I saw where each fifth generation sorcerer before me signed the pages just inside the front. I did this myself when my family had presented it to me on my fourteenth birthday. It had been a big deal, with my parents throwing a get-together and everyone celebrating the occasion. I smiled at the memory, but shook my head to bring my focus back to my task.

I leafed through the pages, looking for something to forbid me from doing this. I really didn't want her to die, so I had to make sure it was safe first. Of course, her falling in love with someone else would be as hard on me emotionally. Regardless, I wanted Livvie to live a long, full life.

The book was full of spells that were special to our family. Spells that had been used in defeating powerful beings in the past. There was information about our war with vampires a few centuries ago. The race of beings had been brutal when first created, many of them killing and exposing their nature at every corner. It was then the council was created, to prevent the different beings from putting all of us in danger. No one knew why we existed, we just did, but if anyone found out it all could be put in jeopardy.

There was even a chapter on how to survive if you met your heart mate at thirteen, like my great-great-great grandmother had. I riffled through the pages, careful not to rip any, to find the information about our curse, the details on what could happen and what could not. There were at least fifty dedicated to the subject, so I decided to just study the passages until it was close to time for her to sleep...then I could see her.

OLIVIA

I was lying in my oversized bed, with the fluffy covers pulled up to my face and my eyes closed, trying to drift off to sleep. Only, sleep wouldn't come to me. I was worrying about school tomorrow. What was I going to do when Aiden tried to prove himself to me? I tossed to the other side. Why did I care so much? And why did I say yes to his invitation? Staring out the window, I noticed how the stars were so mesmerizing. If only life could be as simple as the stars in the sky. Simply being, surviving, even thriving, without all this stress. They would always be in the sky, but people...well people were not that predictable. I closed my eyes yet again, willing myself to sleep.

The familiar sensation of my dreams engulfed my body. It was like I was floating... but not. I felt completely safe, yet I didn't even know where I was. I looked around, realizing the dream was new this time. I usually started out kissing Mr. Sexy, but this time I was in a room by myself. Looking around, I noticed it was familiar from previous dreams. It was the normal medium bedroom size, with dark blue walls. By the door on the far wall sat a desk with two computer screens and lots of office supplies. A shelf with a ton of ancient looking books sat next to the desk. The bed I was resting on had a bedspread the same color as the walls and a few very fluffy pillows. There was a TV with a gaming system by the closet and a window to my left. A window! I leapt off the bed and looked out to see if I recognized where I was. I was taking it all in when I heard something—or rather, someone—behind me.

I spun and he was already inches from my face. He was so close that I could smell him, and he smelled delicious, like a fresh showered scent with a hint of outdoors. Manly and sexy, in my opinion.

"Where am I? Who are you?" I asked him quietly.

His deep eyes looked into mine. "My Livvie, I can't tell you yet. But I can let you know other stuff about me, if you wish," he said.

His voice was deep and alluring and made me weak in the knees. He had called me his Livvie. No one had ever called me that before.

"Yes! I want to know everything about you, but how do I know you're real? I can't stop thinking about you, and it makes me feel like I'm losing it." I let my voice trail off, hoping he didn't think I was crazy. "Is this real?" I was worried about the possible fake dream guy thinking I was losing it...I truly was.

"Yes," he nodded. "Ok, my Livvie, I am twenty years old. I live in the city next to you, but I don't think you've ever seen me. I fell in love with you when you walked by the coffee shop I was in a little over a year ago. The Triple Perk, on 4th Street. And...this is real, Livvie. All of the dreams truly happen. You are asleep, but I'm actually here with you."

I let it all sink in. This was real. I walked over to the desk and sat in the chair. This was probably the safest place for me, so I didn't end up making out with him again. I wanted to, but I also wanted to know what was going on. Ohmygosh, did he say this was real? Clenching my eyes shut, I pinched the bridge of my nose. I'd made out with some dude, for real, in my dreams. We'd kissed, touched, enjoyed each other. I'd practically fallen for him. Opening my eyes, I slowly lifted my head and looked at him.

"So...how does this happen?" I asked him, my eyes desperately searching his.

"Well, my love, it's a very long and difficult story, but you will find out soon. I just wanted you to know they are actually happening. I am in love with you, Olivia Whitehead."

His face lit in excitement, his eyes shining and radiating happiness. And I believed him. This handsome man was really in love with me. What was I supposed to do now? I studied him some more, taking him all in. His dark hair was messy, and he wore jeans and a black buttoned shirt. He looked damned sexy standing there, looking at me like I was the only person in the world. I stood and walked toward him, my hormones controlling my moves. I reached for his face when he grabbed my hand and stopped me.

"Livvie, not tonight. I can't tonight. I won't be able to stop...and...I don't want our first time to be in a dream."

He said it with such disappointment that my heart ached for him. I reached for him again, but he was gone.

Sitting straight up in my bed, sweaty and confused, I fumbled to turn on the light. I massaged my temples with my fingers, trying to figure out what was wrong with me. He had said it was real, but wouldn't my dreams try to convince me of that? I mean, it was my subconscious. How could I know what was really going on? This was starting to freak me out.

Felicia Tatum

Rubbing my eyes, I glanced around the room and that's when I noticed it—a yellow rose on my dresser. It was beautiful, and it hadn't been there before I went to bed.

Slipping from the bed, I slowly walked to it, fingers extended to feel the velvety softness on my fingertips. Either it was really here or I had reached a new state of insanity. Lifting it, I pressed it to my nose, inhaling the fresh scent. It felt and smelled real. The alarm clock showed the early morning hour, signifying my lack of sleep for the night, and I sighed as I continued staring at the delicate, yellow rose in my hand.

Maybe...just maybe...he was real. And if he was, I didn't know what that meant for me. He said he loved me, but he didn't know me. Was it ridiculous a large part of me hoped he was a real person? Though the rational part of me continued to scream there was no way this was possible, the rose in my palm said otherwise.

What now?

SCOTT

The moment she looked at me with her big green eyes and asked my name, I knew I must leave something for her so she would know I was more than a figment of her imagination. To think she didn't know how real our interactions were, that we truly were together those nights, killed me inside. I longed for the day we could be together. So, I decided to help her along in believing. I noticed when espying that her room had a lot of yellow. I figured it was her favorite color. After I left the dream, but before she woke, I created a Sunshine Daydream rose in her room.

I was lying on my bed, thinking of the events of the night. When espying, our spirits were together. It was enough to calm the hurt in my body from being away from my heart mate, but it wasn't enough for my actual heart. I longed to feel her silky hair under my fingers, to know how soft her lips truly were. I wanted to hear her voice, to be able to hold her in my arms. Why did Livvie have to be so beautiful? And why did that guy have to ask her out? Which reminded me...I got

Felicia Tatum

up and trudged to my computer. I sat so hard in the chair it gave a little squeak like it might break under my weight. It was time to do some research.

Remembering the guy's name was Aiden, I went to Livvie's social networking sites. Maybe they were friends. I was scrolling, getting distracted by pictures of my love, when I saw two guys with the name Aiden. Aiden Cavalier and Aiden Periwinkle. I snickered at the names. One of these guys asked my Livvie to go to the dance and might possibly try to steal her heart. I would just have to listen in while she was at school, so perhaps I could catch a glimpse of my competition. Which reminded me...I needed to ask her about this whole dance thing and if she was definitely going with this jerkwad.

I looked at Cavalier's page. He played sports, ran track, the athletic sort of guy, which probably meant he was a complete idiot. Not that I thought all athletes were idiots; he just looked the type who would have the cocksure, I-am-a-god attitude. He had gray eyes and light brown hair. I knew I was much better looking. Periwinkle, he seemed like one of the brainy kids. He was a year younger than Livvie, so maybe the other guy was the maybe-date...it was driving me crazy not knowing my competition.

How had my family gone through this all these years? Loving someone from afar, knowing at any moments time everything could change. Or worse yet, loving them in daily life only to lose them in a few years. Who was this sorcerer who cast the curse? Why hadn't anyone gone after him and broke it?

Could it be broken?

I turned off the computer and paced around my room. A knock sounded at the door connecting the garage to my parent's house.

"Yeah?" I called out.

46

The door opened and my younger brother, Santos, stuck his head in.

"Yo, can I come in?"

I nodded and he slid in, his hand still on the doorknob. My nose caught a waft of something baking.

"I found out some info on the descendant. The actual sorcerer who set the curse was Devlin Hart. I have a lead now. Just wanted you to know."

"Awesome, San. Thank you so much for helping me, bro. Is everything going ok with you? What are you doing up so early?"

"Yeah, not much going on lately. There is this girl at school I've been competing with. It's a little stressful, but I'm determined to be the head of the class. I've been up studying since 4:30a.m."

Our parents had made it very clear we were to learn everything we could and not use our magical abilities to help us out in any way, but Santos was taking it a bit far. Since kindergarten, he studied three times as much as the average student, surpassing his peers and skipping ahead not once, but twice before he reached sixth grade. It was a lot for Sebastian, his twin, to take in and deal with. The two were often compared, which wasn't entirely fair in my opinion, and Sebastian got the short end of the smart stick.

Nonetheless, Santos didn't treat him any differently and neither did our immediate family, so I supposed that was what truly mattered.

I laughed. "Ok man. Good luck."

He nodded and left, shutting the door with a bang behind him. Santos was short and to the point with most things, never sticking around for small talk. Sometimes I wondered if he could even wrap his brain around it. There was no point to it, no reason behind talking for the heck of it, and Santos always needed a reason for something. He was as rational as rational could be.

Standing, I stretched my arms above my head, feeling the muscles pull. It felt so good after dreamwalking all night. Walking to the window, I saw the first glimpses of the rising sun and sighed. I never felt like I slept well anymore, and while I didn't care, my body seemed to. Closing the curtains, I trudged my way back to my bed. After I undressed, I slid in between the covers and attempted to shut my mind off from this terrible day. This damned curse could cost me my love. If only...my grandmother wouldn't be happy, but I knew I had to find the descendant of Devlin Hart. It couldn't be anyone nice...but...no, I couldn't think about that. I would just have to find the descendant so I could be with Livvie before someone stole her away. I turned off the light and got into bed, knowing I would dream of my Livvie.

OLIVIA

The yellow rose I spun around in my hand smelled like a delicate piece of heaven. Once I saw the flower, I knew he was real. I still didn't know his name, but he said I would soon. Sleep eluded me since I woke from the dream in the early hours of the morning. So I was sitting and staring out at the moon that was going to bed and a sun that was waking. The colors were swirling together and creating a magnificent view. The dark met the light and there was a heavenly orange-yellow glow across the sky.

My front row seat for the sunrise was a window seat in my room with yellow pillows thrown around it. I begged my parents to put it in when I was fourteen, and they finally agreed on my sixteenth birthday. It took quite a bit of remodeling to accomplish, so I was grateful that they finally said yes to it. It was my favorite place to sit and think. The rest of my room reflected my tastes, though not overly decorated. My full-sized bed held lots of fluffy pillows and a cozy yellow comforter. Flopping down on it made me feel like I was on a cloud that magically erased my worries. My dresser was large, but not nearly enough to hold all of my clothing. The closet was full of shoes, clothes, and boxes of stuff that I couldn't bear to throw out from my childhood. I had a small TV on the dresser, with a furry clock beside it. Mornings need something like a furry clock to make them bearable. Glancing over, I saw it said 5:13 in the morning. School would be fun today, though leaving my little sanctuary was difficult on most days. At least it was Wednesday. We had a half day today and the rest of the week off for teacher work days. It was like a mini school vacation before our summer break.

Tonight was my sleepover with Juniper. I always looked forward to them, because we had so much fun together. Our parents had known each other for so long that they let us have sleepovers on school nights sometimes, though this was technically our weekend.

Arrow Rock High, in Arrow Rock, Tennessee, was as small as small could get. We barely had enough people to have a sports team, but we made it work. Everyone knew your business, though. It was quite unfortunate. It seemed like no one could go for a drive without the whole town knowing. My school had roughly 800 students, including those in junior high. My class had 60, tops.

I'd been crazy to think he was from here. I would have known who he was, and remembered him. He was totally gorgeous, so there was *no way* I could ever forget him. He said he lived in the next town...but that could be three different places: Loudon Heights, Kaysville, or Stone. His house might be in any of them. I sat up a little straighter, thinking back to when I was staring out of his window, trying to remember if I recognized anything. It was definitely in a familiar town, but I didn't know which one. There had been a lot of trees, but also houses near his. If only I had thought to look at an address on one of the mailboxes.

Was it crazy to think about a man I dream about like this? A man claiming to have powers, at that. I hadn't even met him, yet there was this pull to him. I longed for his hand in mine, to be able to really look in his eyes. A small part of me couldn't help but think I was crazy to fall for someone I was dreaming about. That just screamed insanity. Maybe someone should call the white coats to come and get me, because there was definitely something wrong with me. Sighing, I looked at the clock again, 6:45 a.m. Time had flown and I needed to get ready for school.

I stood and headed for the closet, thinking of what I might wear today. It seemed like it would be rainy, so I should find something cute but water resistant. I decided on dark skinny jeans with a dark pink off-the-shoulder top, with my hair in a low pony tail. Rain always made my hair look awful, so I had learned to put it up on those days.

I rarely applied a ton of makeup, but I felt the urge to today. After some consideration, I put neutral shade on my lids with dark liner all around and finished with a cat eye look. I gently brushed my face with powder and put a touch of light pink gloss on. I gazed in the mirror and thought that I looked really good in dark pink. It really complemented my skin. I wasn't the overly confident type, but I knew when I looked good, and I felt good that day.

I went back to the closet and shuffled through the boxes of shoes, looking for my black rain boots with polka dots. I found them, but not before a few boxes knocked me on the head. I pulled on the boots and grabbed my book bag, ready to eat breakfast. My phone chimed with a text from Aiden. I stopped in my tracks as I read what it.

"I'm coming to take you to school. I have breakfast in the car. 5 minutes."

I couldn't believe he was actually trying to prove himself to me. And just assuming I would be ok with him taking me to school? Who did he think he was? Before I could get the reply typed, I heard honking outside. Apparently Aiden was here, and he couldn't be bothered to come to the door or wait for a reply.

I walked to his vehicle with purpose, and maybe a bit of sassiness. I cocked my head to the side and stood at the door. If this was his idea of wooing me, it wasn't working. He stared at me, his eyes moving appreciatively up and down my body. I still didn't reach for the door. I was waiting for him to get out and open it. He just showed up like this and couldn't even be a gentleman? Nope. Was not going to happen with me.

After five minutes of staring at each other, he hopped out of his side, saying, "What are you doing, Whitehead? Get in the car."

"No."

His eyes widened. "Why not?"

"Because. You can't just come here without asking and then expect me to just hop in your jalopy."

"Oh."

Coming over, he reached around me and his arm brushed against mine. His closeness made me nervous, and I wanted to move away from him, but there wasn't anywhere to go. He opened the door and bowed with an extravagant flourish.

I couldn't help but laugh when he said, "My lady."

"Thank you, Cavalier," I said with a giggle.

The White Aura

We got settled, and he pointed to a breakfast platter from the only restaurant in town. He gave me a mischievous grin and told me that we were eating at school. I couldn't figure him out. This Aiden wasn't really like the one I knew at school. He was different. I wasn't sure if I liked it or not.

SCOTT

I always had an out of body feeling when I espied others who were far away. I tingled all over and felt as if I were floating beside the person I was espying. I lived about twenty-five miles away, so it was like that when I espied Livvie. I glanced at the clock and realized she should be on the way to school. I supposed it wouldn't hurt to see what she was doing.

I sat back in my chair, closed my eyes, and relaxed. I counted to thirty, breathing deeply with each number. Tingling started at my feet and slowly moved up. Before I got to thirty, my whole body was numb and I felt my spirit drifting.

I concentrated on Livvie's face. If I didn't, I could end up anywhere. I heard her voice...and some guy's. It couldn't be her dad; this guy was too young. I drifted closer and closer until my spirit was beside her. She was in a car. I glanced at the driver and was shocked to see the Aiden Cavalier character sitting behind the wheel. I guessed he was her date. But it wasn't his face that shocked me—it was the red glow surrounding his body. He was a sorcerer, too.

The jolt sent my spirit back to my resting form in a flash. I jerked out of the chair and stumbled as I tried to stand. Rising soon after espying was not the best idea, because it took a few minutes for my physical being and spirit to reconnect. I was there, but the full connection hadn't occurred yet. For a few moments, my body was just moving on its own.

I couldn't believe this Aiden guy was a sorcerer. And one with a red aura! All sorcerers had a specific color about them, mainly related to their families, that consumed most of their aura. Most had two dominant shades, with the outer color being a golden yellow and the inner being their family color. The Tabors were green. Bad sorcerers had a red ring where the golden yellow would normally be. But Aiden...his whole aura was red. This could only mean he was a truly evil spirit. And he was with my Livvie.

Shaking, I knew I needed to relax again in order to watch her and make sure she was safe. I stood and paced a few times back and forth, then sat back down on the bed, knees quivering, and tried to calm my mind. I laid my head against the pillow and closed my eyes. Breathing deeply through my nose, I willed myself to stop thinking. I had to put all thoughts out. I went through the process again, this time counting to fifty.

My spirit rested beside her in the school courtyard. She and this evil sorcerer were eating breakfast together. Jealousy spiked, making me shake and breathe heavily. Continuing to watch them, I couldn't figure what he was up to. He was saying stuff not that funny, yet she was laughing. They were talking about a track meet coming up and how he was ready for it. It apparently was the last one of the year, before summer break. He didn't mention the dance.

I saw in his eyes that he enjoyed looking at Livvie, but I also saw something more. His actions made me believe he knew I was present. Perhaps he sensed the magical surge when I joined. There was an element in the way he stared making me feel uneasy. He kept looking toward where my spirit rested, but didn't seem to know where exactly I was. Possibly because Livvie was sitting with him and he was distracted with not wanting her to know. He was a red sorcerer and would not do something stupid to let his secret out. I was worried about her safety, but the bell rang for class, to my relief. He wouldn't do anything with witnesses around. I started to drift back to my corporeal self, knowing I must speak with my family immediately.

My eyes slowly opened as my spirit returned. I sat while the numbness went away. I learned the hard way to not walk much when I was in such a state. It made for some bruises and broken bones. The first time I espied, I hadn't realized I needed to take things slowly. I had stood too quickly and tripped over a chair, breaking my arm in two places. That had been enough of a lesson for me to take my time ever since.

I stood cautiously and walked toward the bookcase to search for the family history book I'd looked at the day before. I located it and flipped to the index, searching for red sorcerers. I recalled seeing the pages when I was younger, I just couldn't remember where. Maybe it was my nerves, or maybe it was lack of concentration, but now I couldn't find anything. I grabbed the book, plus a few others, and called Grandma. I told her I was in desperate need of her knowledge, and I would be there in a flash. If anyone would know how to help me, it would be her.

OLIVIA

Do you ever get the feeling you aren't alone? Sometimes I felt like someone was watching me. Not in a creepy way, though, more like I sensed a presence. I couldn't really explain the feeling. I just knew I wasn't alone all the time. Occasionally, the impression was so strong that I was convinced if I reached my hand out, I could touch a face. I hadn't tried to do it yet, mainly because I felt this way when people were around me, like this morning during my breakfast with Aiden.

Glancing at the clock, I realized there were only twenty-two minutes of school left. The day slowly trudged along, the clouded sky making for a depressing and dreary day. Sighing, I doodled on my paper and thought back to this morning. Aiden had been very strange. He wanted me to like and approve of him, almost desperately. I wasn't sure what was going on, but something didn't feel right.

In the car, he had been trying way too hard. He said all the right things, but they just seemed…wrong, well, coming from him anyway. Did he expect me to believe he had a sudden interest in art and all of my favorite movies? The boy was as dense as they come. There was no way he understood art, and I loved chick flicks, but what guy would admit that freely?

Breakfast had been easier, because he hadn't seemed to be as nervous. He was more natural. I still wasn't sure what to think of it all. I needed to talk to Juniper. Even though she was all, Oh, Aiden and swoony over the idea, she was my best friend and if I could get her past the excitement of it, I knew she'd listen. The bell rang, and I set out to find J.

I hopped up to her locker, hitting the door with my fist. She jumped in surprise and smothered a scream. It made me laugh, like always, that she got scared so easily. And her reactions made it an easy decision to keep scaring her. "What's up, J?"

"Nothing, Liv. I'm getting my stuff so we can go par-tay," she said with a wide grin. She fidgeted with the hem of her shirt and bit her lip as she stared me down.

"Ok, I have to talk to you about something important on the way to your house."

"Important? Oh, come on, noooooo! Not today. It's sleepover night. Important can wait," she said with a wave of her hand, as if she were just wiping the conversation away.

"J, listen. This is really important. Aiden is giving me weird feelings. Something isn't right, and I don't know what to do," I said in an urgent whisper. I didn't want him to overhear.

She looked at me, her eyes wide and confused, and nodded. We walked to her car in silence. I was afraid he would overhear if we talked about it before we were in the safety of her vehicle. I climbed in the passenger seat, waiting until she was in before looking at her.

"Ok, Liv, what do you mean by bad feelings? He makes you want to throw up, or there's some internal alarm system going off?"

"An alarm. I feel like he's trying really hard to make me like him, but I don't know why. He just showed up at my house this morning with breakfast, which was kind of sweet, but how did he know where I live? And he just kind of expected me to fall at his feet because he showed interest in me..." I trailed off. I didn't know how else to explain letting that I really was kind of unsure about this whole situation, but couldn't base it on anything more than a feeling.

"I told him I would probably go to the dance with him when he called last night, J." She squealed at that one. "But now I don't know if that was the best idea. What if he thinks we're dating? I barely know him."

"Liv, calm down. First, I can't believe you said yes and didn't call and tell me. Second, I know I was all for Aiden yesterday, but something happened today. I don't know about this dance either. I overheard him talking outside of the bio lab this morning. He didn't know I was at my locker." She looked at me, her big brown eyes full of concern.

I didn't think this was something I wanted to hear. "First, I said probably, and second, what did he say, J?"

"Well, he was on his phone...he kept saying 'She is the one, and she will be the one to free Delana.' Now I don't know who in the hell Delana is, but if he likes you, he needs to move on from this chick."

She was getting into her overprotective mode. Now I was really worried. J didn't act like a guard dog unless things were serious, and she thought this was.

"Delana...do we have anyone at the school named Delana?"

"No, I already checked. I can't find anyone by that name on his friend pages, the yearbook, or anywhere. The name is just up in the air. I don't want him to hurt you, though, Liv. You deserve so much better than someone hung up on another girl," she threw her hands up in defeat.

"Let's just go to your house. We can talk about this more. I think he's watching us." And he was. I could see him in J's mirror. We were sitting in her little BMW. Did I mention her parents are very generous? He was standing two rows away from the parking spot, slouched against his Jeep and just staring at Juniper's car. It almost felt like he was staring right at me.

"Let's get far away from Mr. Popular/Stalker/Potential Creeper," she said as she put the car in reverse.

"J, I don't know what to do," I said as I glanced in the rearview mirror. I was worried that he would follow us. Not that it mattered. He already knew where I lived, thanks to our small town. So I doubted it would be difficult for him to find Juniper's house, considering she was just two streets over.

"Well, I'm going with you. Mark and I will double date with you. I don't want you alone with him."

Mark was our guy friend/guy she liked. He was a geeky type, on the debate team and a Star Wars fanatic. He was tall with dark hair and green eyes. He was also very muscular, like he worked out a lot. Personally, I thought he was really attractive, and J needed to just date him already. But she was worried about ruining friendships and awkward moments. I was hoping the dance would change that for them.

"Wait a minute...you and Mark?" I asked with a sly grin.

She blushed and nodded. It took about two seconds for me to start bouncing up and down in my seat, squealing with delight. It took about two more seconds for her to do the same.

"Details. Now."

"Ok, ok. He came over to study last night, and I just casually mentioned that I wanted to go and didn't want to go alone. He was quiet for a few minutes and then asked if I wanted us to go together. Ohmygosh, Liv, he seemed nervous! Maybe he does like me," she said, her voice rising with excitement.

"I've been telling you that for forever now, J. If you'd only listen to me," I said with a punch to her arm.

"Hey! No hitting, I have to look rockin' for the dance."

"Oh, like that did anything to your arm," I said with another punch.

"Stop it, Olivia Myla Whitehead," she shouted at me.

We burst into giggles. She sounded like a parent using my full name.

"Ok, ok. You win. I'll let you look hot and stuff for the dance. Are you going to tell him you like him?"

"Maybe. Depends on what happens. I want him to tell me first, Liv."

"I get that. I think he will," I said with a wide smile. I had thought Mark had the hots for her since sophomore year, but she wouldn't listen to me.

My phone rang, distracting me from the moment. I looked down and saw it was Aiden. We were pulling into her driveway, and I declined the call. I wasn't even sure what to say at this point. Just so I wasn't rude, I sent a quick text saying I was with a friend and couldn't talk. Still, I glanced around as I stepped out, expecting him to be waiting behind one of the bushes or something weird like that. "J, he just called."

She looked as worried and confused as I felt when we walked to the house. Something about this whole situation felt *wrong*. I kept saying and thinking that, but I had no idea why. The off feelings only surfaced when I was away from him. When we spent time together, the dread and uneasiness wasn't apparent at all. We went to the kitchen and made a snack—crackers with grapes and cheese. I looked at J. Today, she was wearing glasses, but they were clear lenses. She thought they made her look smarter. Her hair was pinned back on the sides, and her earrings were her signature quarter notes.

I knew I needed to decide what to do about Aiden. Either way, I was going to the dance, but I wasn't sure how to handle the situation. Plus, I needed to talk to Aiden about his creepiness.

Juniper interrupted my thoughts. "We need to buy dresses," she said through a mouthful of grapes.

"Tomorrow. We'll go to Anna's tomorrow. You have to get something totally sexy for your night with Mark," I said with a wink.

She threw a grape at me, her mouth open wide in shock as she fumbled to keep her chewed grapes in.

"We won't be doing anything like that, Olivia," she shouted.

"J, I know that. I'm just playing. Anna's tomorrow. Sexy dress so you can drive him crazzzzzy."

The White Aura

Our giggles were back, and I knew it was going to be a great sleepover.

Anna's was the dress shop in the next town, Loudon Heights. Anna was an older lady, about fifty or sixty, and the sweetest person ever. I loved going to her boutique because she always had some sort of baked good for customers. And we knew we could find the perfect outfit for any occasion at her place. I had to remember to call and ask my dad for some money when he got home from work.

SCOTT

Aiden was evil. If Grandma was right, and I was guessing she was, he had been around for a long time and possessed a bad record. In all of our family books, there was only one sorcerer with a completely red aura. In his beginning days, they called him the Crimson Calamitous. Born over a thousand years ago, he had destroyed over 200 sorcerers and two council homes. Our council was between ten to twenty older sorcerers. They lived in a discreet location, guarded by protection wards, curses, and a plethora of other security measures surrounding the home. The often moved around, keeping safe from the dangers out there. It was almost impossible to get in the building, but it had been accomplished. Twice. The red sorcerer was dangerous. Now it was possible he was here and after Livvie. My head hurt thinking about it.

The Crimson Calamitous never had an actual name in the legends, but he did have a lover, Delana. She was killed by one of the family members of a sorcerer he murdered. This powerful and evil sorcerer could conjure anything he wanted, withstand the powers of a whole clan, and change himself into any form. He possessed a multitude of powers, and after Delana was murdered, he went crazy. He vowed revenge. After killing everyone he could, he disappeared for quite some time. He hadn't been heard of in years, but now here he was. And I was seeing him.

The clock said it was almost midnight. Livvie should be sleeping soon, so I needed to get ready to go to her. No talking tonight. She asked way too many questions last night. I decided to espy her first to make sure she was asleep. Relaxing on my bed, I leaned my head against the wall and breathed in deeply, concentrating on her bright green eyes and wavy red hair.

"Juniper, stop."

Livvie was shouting at her friend, who had a camera in her hand. Livvie was in a tank top and pajama pants with horses on them. They apparently were having a sleepover and decided to put that green stuff on their faces. I deciphered that Juniper was trying to get pictures for future blackmailing purposes.

"I won't show anyone. I just need it for...ya know...fond memory purposes," Juniper said as she darted around.

In seconds, she was in Livvie's face and clicked the camera twice, blinding her and stopping her from turning away.

"Juniper Grace Parks, I can't believe you just did that," Livvie yelled as she dove at her, trying to grab the camera.

Getting to see Livvie in this environment was entertaining. The doorknob turned and a young face poked its way in. The girl looked a little like Juniper, with longer hair. She was probably thirteen or so, I guessed.

"Guys...mom is going to wake up if you don't be quiet," the girl said.

She looked around, trying to figure out what caused the commotion.

"Chelsea, why aren't you in bed?" Juniper asked in a bossy voice.

"Because you two woke me up."

Silence. Livvie looked uncomfortable and Juniper annoyed. Livvie started toward her, putting her hand out to Juniper in a way that said: stop, I'll handle her. "Sorry, Chels. We didn't mean to wake you up. We'll be quieter from now on, ok?"

Chelsea nodded. She gave one last look around. It seemed to me she wanted to be included, but knew she was too young. She closed the door softly behind her.

"She drives me crazy, Liv."

"Oh, J, she just looks up to you. Stop it. We should include her next time."

"We'll include her when she stops running to tell my parents every single thing we say or do."

I decided this was a good time to leave. My spirit slowly returned to my body. I forgot about leaning my head back and bumped it against the wall with a thud. Rubbing the spot with my hand, I picked up my textbook to study a bit before Livvie went to sleep.

Two hours later, my brain hurt from studying the history of Spain. Frustrated with the classes I was taking, I promised myself to decide on a major this semester. I closed my book, throwing it in the floor beside my bed. I flipped the light

switch and lay back, exhausted and wanting to see Livvie. I
said the spell allowing me to dream walk:

In a state to not be disturbed

I walk and exist as I am in life

Take me to the land of her dreams

Where things stay the way they seem

*My eyes began to close. The spell put me into a deep
trance. I could feel myself in Livvie's room. She was lying in
her bed in a blue nightgown. I lay beside her. Her wide green
eyes opened, and a smile spread across her lips. I leaned in
and kissed her softly, my teeth tugging at her lips and my
tongue exploring her mouth. A low moan escaped her and
sent my mind reeling. My hands caressed her thighs, and she
grasped at my chest. Heat flooded my body as my need for
her grew stronger and stronger.*

"Livvie," I whispered softly in her hair.

*Soft hands tugged at my pants, trying to free my body of
them. Eyes full of need gazed deep into mine, and I knew I
must stop her. I couldn't make love to her like this. My lips
found her neck and kissed and sucked on velvet skin. Sharp
nails suddenly sunk deeper into my shoulder muscles, and
teeth bit down on my lips. When she released her grip, my lips
trailed my way to hers. She kissed me deeply. I knew I had to
go now. The need for her was too much. I took one last
longing look at her.*

I came out of the trance slowly. My surroundings were
fuzzy at first, but my room gradually became visible. I woke
up in the floor. I always came to in different locations within
my apartment after our expeditions. My body was still aching
for Livvie. Her touch had lit every inch of me on fire. I glanced

at the clock, noticing I was in the dream for almost two hours. It felt like five minutes.

I walked to the bathroom, rubbing my shoulder along the way. She really dug her nails in. After turning on the light, I pulled my shirt off to look. Deep scratches started at my shoulder blade and went up to my neck. Those were gonna hurt when I showered. I stripped off the rest of my clothing and turned the water on cold. I needed to relax my mind and reduce the heat simmering inside me. A cold shower was the perfect remedy, and hopefully the cool stream of water wouldn't burn my love wounds.

OLIVIA

Sleepovers with Juniper felt like wild parties, well, for us anyway. We watched movies, ate a lot of junk food, and talked non-stop. Last night had been a night of facials, music, and musicals. We talked a little about the Aiden situation, but I still wasn't sure what I was going to do. The conversation revolved mostly around Mark. Juniper had liked him since we were twelve or so.

He was in our class and became friends with us during an assembly one day. There was a kid in our class—Rob—who was always picked on by the popular kids. He was really small then. Scrawny and pimple faced, but at twelve, most kids were. At the assembly that cold winter morning, Rob sat in the far corner of our section. He tried his hardest to ignore the bullies. The most popular guy in the class, Kevin, walked up to Rob's seat and started picking on him. Juniper and I moved closer to him, trying to deflect the attention, but it didn't work. Kevin kept on and on, making fun of everything from Rob's face to his parents' vehicles.

That's when Mark stepped in. He was still new. He had just moved to Arrow Rock that previous fall. He sat beside Rob and looked Kevin straight in the eye. His voice didn't waver at all when he said, "That's enough. There's no need to make fun of someone else to make yourself feel better." We all were friends after that. And Rob? Well he wasn't scrawny and nerdy anymore, and most of the kids who bullied him wanted to be his friend now.

I rolled over and glanced at the clock: 8:00 a.m. Way too early for any day that we didn't have school, but J and I had dresses to buy. I shook her. She didn't budge. Juniper was a heavy sleeper, and this was the worst part of sleepovers.

I shook her again. "Juniper."

She groaned a little and rolled over. I was a very light sleeper, so it was frustrating to wake someone else. I heard Mrs. Parks in the hall. Maybe she could bring me a water bottle to throw on J.

"Hey, Mrs. Parks, how do I wake your daughter?" I called out.

This got to Juniper. She sat straight up and looked like she could kill me.

"Don't say that to her. She'll bring ice water or an air horn or something ridiculous like that," she said sleepily.

"Ha ha. Well, get up, sleepy head. We've got clothing to try on."

"Ok, ok." She groaned and fell down, throwing the pillow over her head.

I crawled to the floor, creeping to her head under the pillow and yelled, "Juniper!"

She jumped, smacked me with the pillow, and sulked to the bathroom.

I threw on jeans and a black tank top. I didn't bother with makeup and left my hair naturally wild and wavy. Before I was finished, J came back and silently got dressed. She would wake up once we started driving. She just couldn't come awake and talk at the same time.

"Ok, I'm ready, Miss Early Bird Sunshine."

I smiled and grabbed my bag, "Ok, then let's go."

"Breakfast on the way?"

"Of course, J. You pick, though."

"Mmk."

It was a twenty minute drive to Loudon Heights. We stopped and bought biscuits and gravy. J's silver BMW glided along the road to the town. The trees were coming alive in the spring weather, like a fire fed gasoline. Something about nature was so calming. Seeing the growth in spring made me want to go to an empty field, far away from everyone and everything. Breathing in the fresh air, feeling soft grass between my toes, smelling the fresh flowers...nature was the best place to meditate.

Lost in my own thoughts, I didn't notice Juniper pulling into Anna's parking lot. The building was white with big windows on the sides to display dresses. Blue, green, yellow, and pink gowns lined the windows. Prom and dance season was in full swing. Any passerby could tell by looking at the building. We opened the door and were greeted by a chiming bell. We immediately smelled freshly baked cupcakes and brownies.

"Hello, ladies," Anna said as she came from the back room.

71

Felicia Tatum

Wearing a long brown skirt and a royal blue shirt, she looked wonderful. The top's color perfectly matched her eyes. She was short, with hair that was beginning to gray. Something about her was just so warm and kind. I loved shopping here.

"Miss Anna," we both exclaimed together and went to hug her.

She had always been like a grandmother. Our mothers brought us here when we were little girls to get our holiday attire.

"What are you ladies here for today?"

"Well, we have a spring dance we're going to, and we both have to have new dresses. We want to look our best," Juniper said giving her the biggest smile imaginable.

"Oh, a dance. How exciting. Well, I have a great one in mind for you, young lady," she said to Juniper.

We walked around the racks to a black dress. It was gorgeous. Long and strapless, with a slit over the leg. On either side of the slit, there was a silver trim of little diamonds. It came with elbow length gloves with a matching trim around the top. It screamed Juniper and was almost as beautiful as her.

"J, you have to get that one. It's so lovely and perfect for you," I said while admiring the wonder in front of me.

"I'm going to try it on," she said.

She was holding it out in front of her to admire while walking to the fitting curtain.

"Now, for you..." Miss Anna let her voice trail off as she looked around.

The White Aura

Her sight stopped on a white dress across the room. It was knee length, with tulle underneath the skirt. It kind of looked like an upside-down teacup around your waist. The top was sleeveless, with bunched silk on the shoulders. The material went out and down into a V, landing below the breasts and going halfway down the back. My breath caught in my throat. The fabric called to me, the softness caressing my fingers. It was sexy, but not too sexy, and very girly.

"Well, I can tell by the look on your face that you like it too. Let's get it so you can try it on," she said with a big smile on her face.

As we were walking across the shop, Juniper came out. She looked drop dead gorgeous. Her face was lit up; she knew she looked beautiful. "This is it," she said with excitement in her voice.

She picked out some matching silver heels, and that made her quite a bit taller. I took my choice and went behind the curtain. I stripped down to my panties, taking my bra off as well to get the full effect. I pulled the dress over my head and gasped. It fit perfectly and made me look like I was curvier than I truly was. Juniper and Anna both looked at me, eyes and smiles wide when I stepped out from behind the curtain.

"It's perfect," they both exclaimed at the same time.

I laughed and walked to look in the multi view mirror. The shape accented my breasts and legs perfectly. It was official. I was in love with the amazing fabric. I spun a few times, feeling like a kid in her first puffy frock. Giggling, I walked to the shoes and picked out a coral pair with a lovely bow on the top. The heel on them wasn't too tall but enough to lift me at least two inches. I grabbed them and went to change back.

As we purchased our gowns and shoes, I noticed some beautiful flowers behind the counter.

"Oh, Anna, those flowers...where did you get them?" I asked. Something about them seemed familiar, as crazy as it seemed. They were flowers, for goodness sake. I could find them on the side of most roads.

"Oh, they're from my garden. I just love blossoms. They're such fun to grow," she said, as she smiled at me. "It'll be $242.55 for you, Olivia, and $255.87 for you, Juniper."

We gave her our parents' debit cards, making small chit chat as she rung us up. She wrapped our packages, and we sat to snack on her desserts.

"Olivia, I think you should meet my grandson," Miss Anna said sweetly.

"Oh, really? Why do you think that?" I froze, convinced she was going to try to set me up.

I glanced at Juniper for help. She just shrugged her shoulders.

"Well, he's very sweet and handsome. I think you two would get along well."

"Maybe I will soon," I said with a smile in her direction.

I didn't have any other events anytime in the near future, so perhaps she would forget about it before I saw her again.

"Miss Anna, these brownies were delicious, but we have to get going. Our parents will expect us home soon," Juniper said as she decided to come to my rescue.

"Oh, of course, my dears. Please take pictures of you two at the dance. I would love to see them," she said as she hugged each of us.

"We will," we agreed as we took our purchases. We walked to the car, ready to go back to Juniper's house.

SCOTT

I helped my grandma at her dress boutique on Thursday mornings and weekends. When I turned eighteen, I decided to get a job. My parents, the strict people they were, demanded all of their children to live life as mortals in many ways, including saving for things we could easily conjure. A car was out of the question to them, so a job was a necessity. I wanted to look for one when I was in high school, but my parents wouldn't allow it. After looking around town for some time, I went to her to talk about it. She felt sorry for me and needed some help, so we decided I would help out in the back. I unloaded boxes and arranged fabrics and supplies.

She was ancient, so she had picked up a few hobbies in her time. She opened the store because it was her most recent favorite. She actually made all of the clothing. Some of them were from years ago, while some of them were recent creations. Either way, people seemed to love her shop. She had been open for the past fifteen years. In order to deflect people questioning her age, she actually dyed her hair with bits of gray as the years passed. The things we had to do as sorcerers to prevent humans from finding out were magnificent.

Today, I was running late. I had overslept after the dreamwalking last night. I pulled into the gravel parking lot and almost hit a silver BMW. The silly horn honked and the tires squealed as the driver slid out onto the pavement. My truck almost slammed into the side of the little car. I felt a wave of nausea flash through my stomach as I thought about the potential accident. Parking the car, I laid my head on the steering wheel, wondering just how much worse this day could get.

Regaining my composure, I opened the door and slid out. I went around the back of the building, passing the dumpsters and bales of boxes to recycle. I opened the door and got to work arranging the boxes. She got sewing inventory in on Friday, so on Saturday I always arranged it into categories she had determined.

As I was checking off the inventory list, Grandma came in the doorway, "Little one, we need to talk about the CC." CC was our code name for our evil sorcerer. Too many questions would be asked if someone overheard.

I'd known she would question me. "Don't you have customers, Grandma? One tried to run me down a few seconds ago." I was hoping to deflect her questions. I didn't even look her way.

"They left. Now, come on. Come sit and let us chat." She gently laid her hand on my back and guided me into the shop.

The check-out counter was covered in bags and flowers, the racks filled with gowns of all varieties. The shoe section was on the right side of the front door. In the middle of the shop was the area that made the whole place so homey. There, a round table sat loaded with fresh baked goods. This is where she led me to sit and talk. I knew the moment I set foot in the main shop she'd been here. I was hit with the overwhelming feeling of her spirit, felt the calmness only she could bestow.

"Livvie was here," I growled, glancing around. Was she still here? I couldn't meet her now!

"Yes, she's gone. Now focus so we can talk."

Blinking, I stared at her. "You know Livvie?"

She nodded, dismissing the conversation about my heart mate. "Now, little one, you need to listen to me and listen good. The CC is not someone to mess with. If he hurts you, I can't heal you. He has powers unlike any we've ever seen, and it's basically impossible to defeat him. It would take some very powerful and old spells to do it. I'm not sure why you were asking, but I suspect it has something to do with Olivia. Is she in danger?"

"Yeah, Grandma, she is. Could be he's in Arrow Rock."

She stared at me, her eyes as wide as saucers. "Here?"

"Yes. I saw someone while I was espying Livvie...his aura was completely red." I looked at her desperately.

I needed her to believe me and help.

"You're sure? All red? Maybe the inner was pink?"

She was trying to think of alternatives, but she knew I saw him. Her eyes conveyed the fear only an immortal, evil sorcerer could create. Fear wasn't something I think I'd ever see in my grandmother, but she had it. Her breathing intensified as she simply stared at me, the questions running through her mind, though she asked nothing else.

"No, Grandma, no." I shook my head.

"Go back to work. We'll talk more later."

I slowly lifted myself out of the chair, skidding the legs on the hardwood floor. I placed my hand on her shoulder for just a second and walked to the storage room. Looking back for a moment, I saw her still sitting there with hands folded and eyes staring into space. I knew she was trying to think of a plan to protect us all. But also, she was worrying about my involvement. I walked on quietly so I wouldn't disturb her thoughts.

The mirrors were cleaned and everything looked dusted already, so today would consist of stock organizing. I grabbed my clipboard. At the pallets of boxes, I continuing opening each one and checking off what we received. Then I placed it in the appropriate container. As my body worked, I still couldn't redirect my thoughts from Livvie. Her face flashed in my head. I wanted to hold her. To know she was safe, and she wasn't falling in love with someone else. I couldn't make Livvie fall for me, or she would die in roughly ten months and I couldn't fight the CC without knowing how. It left me feeling lost and discouraged. I took my frustrations out on the heavy boxes needing to be crushed.

OLIVIA

I was outside. The moon was high and shining, creating a glow around the trees surrounding me. This was a new location. I looked around for Mr. Sexy...but I couldn't see him anywhere because it was too dark. I realized this place was familiar. Wait...I was in the field I was daydreaming about earlier. The soft green grass was silk between my toes. There were yellow daisies everywhere, and trees lined the perimeter. I felt like I was in a box. I wore only shorts and a camisole, but I wasn't cold. The wind blew just enough to ruffle my hair.

"Hello?" I called timidly. I was answered with complete silence. Not even the birds were chirping. I glanced around and walked forward. My arms wrapped around the front of me, not for warmth but comfort.

I knew I was dreaming, but this was still kind of scary. There was a deer to my left, simply watching me. She was beautiful and majestic. She came toward me the moment I wished I could pet her. My hand slowly reached out and touched her coarse coat. Huge brown eyes looked into mine. There was no fear.

"You're lovely," I whispered.

"So are you," a deep voice said from behind me.

I turned violently, scaring the deer off into the trees. Mr. Sexy was standing five feet in front of me. Jeans and a fitted white t-shirt clothed his fit body.

"You're here."

"Of course I am, where else would I be?"

"I thought...well, I wasn't sure if this was our dream or just mine."

"It's ours, Livvie. It's ours. Always ours."

"Can I know your name or do I need to keep calling you Mr. Sexy?"

"Keep calling me Mr. Sexy. I like that."

The completely adorable grin on his face was too much for me. I took three steps and jumped in his arms.

"I want to meet you in person. Assuming you're real, that is."

"You know I am, and you will. It's...complicated. But, Livvie...you have to be careful. You could be in danger."

I slid down his body, standing again.

"Danger?"

"Yes. I can't tell you much, but just be careful. With people at school and in town…"

He knew something I didn't.

"Any specific person?"

"Yes, of course. But I can't tell you any more, Livvie. It could put you in even more danger, love."

"Can you tell me what kind of danger? What I should look for? Signs or something…"

"I'll try. This may be difficult to believe, but I'm a sorcerer, Livvie. I have powers. It's how I meet you in your dreams."

He was gauging my reaction. His eyes were cast down and his hands fidgeting. He ran his long fingers through his silky black hair. "I told you before that I would have to wait to tell you everything, but I'm going to go ahead. If…well, if something happens, it won't matter anyway."

I reached up and put my hand on his cheek. He leaned his head in and the look he gave me melted my insides. "I kind of figured something wasn't right when I got the rose. So, go ahead. I'll do my best to trust and believe you."

"There are evil sorcerers in the world. I think one may be after us. I can't meet you in person yet because a long time ago, a curse was set on my family. If we meet the ones we love before they are seventeen and six months, they will die on their eighteenth birthdays. I can't meet you just to lose you, Livvie. Do you understand?" His eyes darted between mine, searching for understanding. What could I say to that?

"So…you meet me and I'll die. You don't meet me, and I could still die because an evil sorcerer is out there and could possibly harm me… or you… or us," I chuckled. "Seriously? And what's with the seventeen and six months? Totally random."

"Livvie, I don't want you to worry, ok? I will take care of it. I'm going to fix the problem, and in October, we will finally meet. I'm in love with you, Livvie. I also have other powers. Sometimes...I come and check on you, just to make sure you're ok. I really, really hope you don't think I'm creepy for doing that."

He did seem to care for me, as absurd as his story was.

"It's not creepy, dream dude. It's kind of romantic. I mean, this hot guy is so in love with me that he visits me in my dreams and checks on me during the day. Wait...why have I never seen you checking on me?" I would have noticed him lurking around.

"Well, it's not my body. It's just my spirit. Kind of like these dreams, it's just my spirit now, too."

His spirit. Well, I really liked his spirit.

"Sit with me?" He smiled and sat in the grass. We lay on our backs, staring up at the sky.

"It's so beautiful out here. Did you know that I was daydreaming about nature today?" I questioned.

"No, but I can tap into your wants. This is where the dream led us. This place is gorgeous. I'm glad you wanted it tonight."

I turned to study him. His face glowed, and his dark hair shone in the moonlight. His facial features were strong: hard cheekbones and jaws with full, pouty lips. His skin was a few shades darker than mine. Maybe he spent a lot of time outside.

"What do you do, Mr. Sexy? Do you have a job?"

"Kind of. I help out my grandma on the weekends and I'm in college. I haven't decided what I want to do with my life, but I know I want you there."

Could he get any more perfect? "What classes are you taking?"

"The basics. Math, English, and a couple of art classes. I like to paint a lot, and I think learning more about it would be fun."

"An artist...makes you even more attractive."

He laughed. It was heavenly, deep, and contagious. "I've painted you, Livvie. Quite a few times actually."

"Can I see?"

"Mmmhmm...I've already left you one. It's under your bed."

"How do you do that?" I giggled as I asked.

"I'm a sorcerer. And a sexy one at that." He raised a brow, giving a wink that made my soul tremble.

We both laughed. We were holding hands. His hand was bigger and much stronger than mine. His fingers were long and the skin rough, but he held my hands tenderly. He seemed afraid he might hurt them if he didn't treat them like something small and delicate. However, our hands fit together perfectly. He looked at me and kissed me. Not a passionate kiss like we usually shared, but a soft, loving kiss, full of promise and hope.

"I have to go now, Livvie. It's almost time for you to wake up."

"Already? Why does our time feel so short?"

"Time while dreaming and real time are quite different, Livvie. Hours of real time are mere minutes in here," he explained. "Please, I need you to be careful. Please watch out for yourself. I'll be on alert as well. I'm researching the evil sorcerer. I will defeat him, and we will be safe, love."

He gave me one last kiss and was gone. I saw the deer again as everything faded from my mind. She was watching me from the edge of the woods.

BEEP! BEEP! BEEP! I slid out of bed and turned the clock off. Stumbling back, I rested on the foot of the mattress. I rubbed my eyes and recollected the dream from last night. The painting. Running around to the side of my bed, I fell on my knees to look under it. There was a 9 by 11 canvas with my face painted on it. It looked so much like me. The strokes weren't even visible. It looked like a photo from a camera. At the bottom, it was signed, "To my Livvie, Love, Mr. Sexy." I rested back on my heels, staring at the painting. My fingers touched the canvas, thinking of how he had painted this with his strong hands. I heard chirping and looked up to see three birds perched outside my window. Their eyes stared into mine like they were trying to tell me something, to warn me of something. Sliding the canvas back under the bed, I went to the window, stopping as the animals fluttered off. At the tree line in the backyard, there stood a deer much like the one from my dream.

Was it possible it was watching me? What was happening?

SCOTT

No one in my immediate family had dealt with the Crimson Calamitous. It worried me, because I hated to put them into any danger. We were very close. My mother and father met when they were in their early twenties, my father a sorcerer and my mother not. I had three siblings: twin brothers who were sixteen and a sister who was fifteen. Santos, Sebastian, and Sadie. I couldn't stand the thought of bringing harm to any of them, but I was going to have to ask for help. If the CC was truly after Olivia, a battle would surely ensue, and Grandma and I couldn't fight alone.

Sadie was talented with charms, so I planned to ask her for protection charms for Livvie. I thought if Sadie put enough around the Whitehead house, Aiden wouldn't be able to go there. Santos was going to be my backup on research. He and Sebastian were awesome students, both of them, surprisingly, though Sebastian didn't try nearly as hard as Santos did. Perhaps Santos would find something I hadn't. Sebastian wasn't as close to the rest of us. He liked to exclude himself from everything. Asking him would probably be a bad idea.

I just wanted to find a way to protect Livvie or save her before the CC did whatever he was planning. That reminded me, I was going to espy him today to see if I could find out anything about his plans.

I sat in my chair and began the techniques. I closed my eyes, relaxed my body, and concentrated on Aiden. It was after school hours, so I was hoping he was in his natural state. I tingled and began to see red. I felt my spirit leaving my body and realized I was in a cave that was lit with an unnatural intensity. There was no doubt that the CC had been here. I smelled something stale, like a moldy piece of furniture sitting around for years. I heard water in the distance. I glanced to my right and noticed him standing over a table made of rock. He was deep in thought reading something. I stepped closer, and his head jerked up. He looked right at me, like he could see me.

"Is someone there?" he asked in a hoarse whisper.

I was undetectable to humans in my spirit state, but I recalled he'd acted strange when I'd espied Livvie, signifying he might sense my presence. There was a strong possibility he knew. I decided I'd better work fast and stepped closer to the table.

He was reading a book that looked older than my grandma. On the left there was a picture of a young girl with red hair just like Livvie's. On the right was text about Delana. It said she was murdered, and since the death was unjust, she could be resurrected if a sacrifice were made. A virgin child, no younger than thirteen but no older than eighteen. My heart began pounding, and my spirit was sucked back.

I jerked home, still tingling and breathing hard. My body landed on the rug beside my door with a hard thump. Was he was going to kill Livvie to resurrect his dead lover? This had to be his plan. Livvie was only seventeen, and I was pretty sure she was a virgin. I thought I was having a panic attack. My chest tightened and it was difficult to breathe.

Santos walked in the room. "Bro...are you ok?"

He got on his knees in front of me, shaking my arms. I couldn't talk. I was too stunned. His dark eyes drove into my soul, like he was trying to get a reading. His main power was empathy, and if he tried hard enough, he could practically read minds. His fingers tightened on my arms, and his nails dug into my flesh. He yelled for our mother and father. I just shook my head. He stared at me for what seemed like hours.

"She's...he's...a virgin sacrifice...."

I couldn't talk in complete sentences. It was obvious he has no idea what in the world I was talking about, but he continued to try to read me. Perhaps it was because I was overwhelmed and my emotions were all over the place, but he seemed to be having a hard time.

"Grandma...call her," I screamed at my parents as they walked in the room.

Sadie came in as well, gifted with a touch of Grandma's healing powers. I began to calm. "Tell me what's wrong, Scottie." Her voice was gentle and concerned.

"Sadie...my Livvie...she's in grave danger. The Crimson Calamitous is after her. He's going to sacrifice her to bring back his dead lover, Delana."

I hadn't told the other members of my family anything about this yet. Only Grandma knew. I could tell by the stunned faces staring at me, they were all shocked. Then everyone seemed to speak at once.

"Did you say the Crimson Calamitous?"

"Who is Livvie?"

"A virgin sacrifice? Have we gone back in time?"

"Are you having an attack?"

"Have you hit your head?"

Questions bombarded me from all directions. Yep, my family members were definitely in shock. Attempting to answer them was fruitless, so I allowed Sadie to continue calming me with her healing effects, the sensation washing over my body in waves, but only working a small amount at a time. Grandma arrived shortly after my family questioned me, and I allowed her to answer them.

I lay back in my seat, resting my eyes from the light. Jerking back so quickly exhausted my body, and I only wanted to sleep so I could connect with Livvie and heal myself.

OLIVIA

Since kindergarten, I had enjoyed going to school. Learning was an integral part of me, my brain soaking as much knowledge as possible to grow and expand what I knew. Living in a small town didn't give me much life experience, and I longed to see all the places I learned about. My classes were small, with me usually ending up in classes with Juniper, and later on with Mark once he moved here. They made the days pass faster. Once we got in high school, I became interested in running track. Running was a fun way to get out of the house, let out steam, and just be free. With everything happening lately, I needed an out. Running was it.

My parents and I weren't as close as other kids and their parents, so getting out as much as possible was a top priority. For as long as I could remember, they worked long hours and weren't home much. If I had a school activity during the day, they were never available to come; but if it was at night, they were there. I knew deep down they cared, but I always wondered why they worked so much. Our home was nice and they didn't seem to be struggling with money. I wasn't sure why I was always put on the back burner.

In fact, I wasn't even sure what they did all day. My mom simply said she was a consultant. When I asked her any questions, the subject always magically changed. My father...well, he was even more secretive about his job. All I knew was he was an important person in an important company...or so they told me.

They had been acting strange lately, even for them. They were gone on the weekends more often, and they were asking me more questions than normal. Mom inquired about my health every day, and they both were watching me, as if waiting for something to happen. Honestly, it made me a little crazy for feeling that way, but I couldn't help it.

So far, it was a boring Friday night. I was sitting home alone, again, waiting for Juniper to come get me. She had asked me to go to a movie with her, but she was picking up Mark first. I hadn't gotten ready, just threw on a long sleeve shirt and jeans. It wasn't quite summer yet, so at night it was still chilly, and movie theaters were known for being cold. Especially the one in Arrow Rock, considering it was a million years old and hadn't been updated since before cars were invented.

As I sat on the couch, I grabbed the home and living magazine my mother left on the coffee table to flip through. Under it was a notebook with elaborate drawings, circles and triangles intertwined underneath the wording. "Binding" was all it said. I tentatively opened it, landing on a random page within.

"Olivia: 11 months to eighteen. No signs of change. No questioning."

Confused, I read it again. My birthday would be in eleven months, but what change was she talking about? And what wasn't I questioning? Before I could ponder anymore, I heard a honk from outside. I slipped the notebook back under the magazine exactly where it was, making a mental note to look again later. It was probably best that mother not know I found her information.

I hurried out into the nippy air. Mark was standing outside the car with the seat already pulled up for me to climb in. Juniper had the heat turned up on high, because she apparently was freezing while the rest of us were simply cool, and I got a face full of hot air when I started in the car.

"Hey, guys," I exclaimed while warming my hands.

"Heeeey, Liv! Are you excited? I'm excited." J's excitement was once again on overdrive and uncontainable.

"Yes, J. I am. I love hanging out with you two," I said with a chuckle. Snapping my seatbelt, I leaned back for the short drive to the theater.

Mark turned to look at me and said, "Well, of course you do. You know why? Because I'm awesome and it makes you two awesome by association."

Juniper playfully punched his arm and swerved the car a little bit.

"J, pay attention," we both yelled in unison.

"Sorry."

I grabbed my phone when I felt it buzz in my pocket. It was a text from Aiden. He said he was bored, so I took a big chance and invited him to the movies with us. "Going to movies with J and Mark. Come if you want." *Omg why did I do that?* Making stupid, spontaneous decisions was my forte lately.

"Sounds good. Meet you there in ten."

I bit my lip as I read his reply. I didn't think he would come, and now I wasn't sure how Juniper would react. Mark had always been friendly, so I didn't think it would be an issue for him. But Juniper was still protective and indecisive about the whole thing.

"Uh…guys?"

"Yeah, Liv?"

Sticking my head between their seats, I blurted out, "I invited Aiden to come with us. Hope that's ok."

The car went silent. Mark glanced at Juniper like he wasn't sure if she was going to explode like a bomb or not. Her hands tightened on the steering wheel making her knuckles pale. I saw her eyes darting around in the mirror. Anxiety crossed her face, but then it all seemed to disappear.

"Ok."

"Ok?"

"Ok."

Mark glanced back at me and gave a little shrug like he had no clue what was going on. I didn't really know either, so I just leaned back for the last few minutes of the car ride.

SCOTT

The Tabors always had "family night" on Fridays. We would watch a movie, go bowling, or find some other activity we could all do together. Tonight, we were all settled at Grandma's house. She, Sadie, and my father were in the kitchen cooking a three-course meal that would be delicious. I could smell some veggies, maybe green beans and carrots. Also, my nose detected some kind of pasta sauce my father was more than likely making from scratch. My mother and I played cards while Santos observed. Sebastian sat in the far chair looking bored. He never really liked to participate in family night. We all tried our hardest to include him in the things we did, but he never seemed interested. No matter how hard we tried, how much we did for him, or how caring we were, Sebastian always seemed to be an outsider.

"Scott," my father yelled from the kitchen, "come here, please."

"Hey, Santos, keep an eye on Mom. Don't let her look at my cards."

"Got it, Captain," he said with a salute.

I jogged into the kitchen and witnessed the worst mess of my life. My sister stood off to the side, trying to hide her giggles, while my grandma stood fuming, staring at my father.

"Uh, Dad?"

"Listen, son, there was a little problem. The sauce was on too high and went everywhere. I need you to run to the store to get a few more ingredients."

I couldn't help but laugh. The white stove top was now covered in red sauce. My father was splattered. My grandma...well she wasn't doused in sauce, but she was red from anger. She hated to let anyone else cook in her kitchen. When something like this happened, she got furious. Which wasn't good, because when sorcerers got upset, their powers could get out of control.

"Grandma? It's ok. We'll clean it up," I said when I regained my composure. Waving my hand, I expelled heat from my palm, wiping everything clean. "See?"

"I told him to turn it down, but did he? Ooooh, no. He said he knew what he was doing, and I needed to leave him alone. He said he had everything under control. He said..." She was cut off by my father putting his hand up to stop her.

"Mom, I said I was sorry. It's cleaned up. Now please calm down before you make the house explode or something."

He turned to take care of the dishes, and stirred the remaining pots on the stove. He nodded at the kitchen table and said the list I needed was there.

"Sadie, you wanna come with?"

"Sure."

I grabbed the list and keys, and we headed toward the front door.

"Hey, Santos, take my place, ok? We have to run to the store."

He nodded and glanced over my cards, checking each one to see what kind of hand he was getting. Just as Sadie and I got to the door, Sebastian called out to us. "I want to go with you."

I stopped dead in my tracks. Sebastian never wanted to go anywhere with me. I couldn't believe what I was hearing, so I turned slowly. "Say that again?"

"I said I want to go with you. Is that ok?"

He had a look on his face that was a mixture of boredom and cockiness.

"Yeah, sure it is, Sebas. Come on," Sadie said as she gave me a look that said "let's see what he's up to." We all walked to my truck in silence and climbed in. I drove us to the store in a cab filled with eerie quiet.

OLIVIA

Aiden was waiting for us when we arrived at the theater. He and Mark exchanged pleasant but short hellos. Mark hadn't voiced it, but he obviously wasn't a fan of Aiden. They had a tension whenever around one another I couldn't explain. It made me uncomfortable. Like now, Aiden stuffed his hands in his pockets, waiting for me to speak, while Mark eyed him carefully. Juniper hadn't said anything to anyone since "Ok." The theater was crowded, and we had to stand in line for what seemed like forever. Aiden paid for my ticket, and we walked to the concessions. Juniper was waiting to order popcorn when I finally decided we had to discuss this before the night was ruined.

"J, will you go to the restroom with me?"

She didn't say anything, only nodded.

We walked away, leaving the boys in line with our orders.

"Are you mad?"

"Kind of. I thought you didn't like him. Now you're inviting him out with us."

"I'm sorry, J," I said as I pushed the door open.

"Do you like him or not? That's all I want to know. I just don't want him to hurt you or him to turn out weird or something."

"I don't think I want to date him, no. But I don't see why we can't be friends. He's been really nice here lately. Besides, I need to talk to him, find out what he thinks is going on and everything."

"Ok, ok. I'll be nice then. Or at least I'll try," she said with a grin on her face.

I shook my head as I laughed, "Thank you so much, J. I know this worries you."

"Yeah, yeah. Let's get back to the boys. I'm not so sure they like each other."

We made our way out of the crowded restroom, giggling about the thought of the boys waiting for us. Making guys wait while girls went anywhere together was fun. It seemed like the male species always commented that girls liked to go places in packs. So feeding the mindset was quite entertaining. Mark and Aiden were standing beside the concessions holding popcorn and drinks. They looked anxious for our return.

"Hey, guys, need a hand?" Juniper asked while sneakily letting her fingers slide over Mark's arm and leaning her body closer to him.

"Yes," Mark said while his eyes moved appreciatively over her.

I knew he liked her. I wondered why he wasn't doing anything about it.

"You gonna help me, Whitehead?"

"Oh, sure," I exclaimed, grabbing the drinks from Aiden's hand.

He gave me a sly grin and a wink as his stride aligned with mine. I was unsure why, but he made me nervous. Yes, he was good looking. Yes, he was a bit intimidating with all his athletic skills, but why did I get butterflies in my stomach around him? I didn't feel much attraction to him, but I couldn't deny there was some. However, in the back of my mind, thoughts of my dream man haunted me, reminding me there may be more waiting for me.

A part of me wondered if the dreams I'd been having were false. Sorcery was pretty extreme...and that curse? If I was making all this up, maybe I needed to consider writing a book. Perhaps I was crazy and wanted someone that badly. But another aspect of me, deep within, knew he was a part of my life. He had given me a rose and a painting. How did that happen if he wasn't real? If the sorcery stuff wasn't real? I just didn't know if I would ever meet him.

"Whitehead?"

I snapped back to the present, gasping from the shock of having to focus on Aiden's face inches from mine. His breath was slow and deep, and his stormy gray eyes were boring into my soul. My heart raced. I gasped a little and stepped back from him. My body was reacting to him, and it scared me. Wanting him wasn't something I could deal with. Why was I reacting this way?

"Yeah," I stammered, trying to break his gaze. My eyes just couldn't seem to move away from his.

"I was talking to you, but it seems like you're in a completely different world. You ok?" he asked with concern. His hand reached out to caress my arm.

I shuddered. "Yeah, fine."

"Ok. Well, Juniper and Mark went in to find us seats. We should probably go in," he said. He opened the theater door for me.

"Wait," I said and put my hand up to stop him.

Turning, he let the door shut. He looked at me patiently, waiting for whatever it was I was going to say.

"I wanted to ask you something, Aiden. How did you know where I live?"

"Everyone knows where you live. It's Arrow Rock, Whitehead," he said with a chuckle.

"So, you aren't stalking me or something?"

"What? No. I thought we were friends," he said sounding disheartened

"Yeah, we are. I just got worried is all. I don't know how I feel about you, Aiden…I don't want to lead you on or anything."

"I know, and it's fine. I told you I would prove myself."

"Ok. Well, let's go in now."

"All right, Whitehead, after you," he said, opening the door wide.

The White Aura

The theater was full—it was Friday night after all—and the closest seats J and Mark could find were two on one row and two on the row below it. That meant we would be divided. My heart was still beating like a drum from the close encounter with Aiden. My palms were sweating a little bit at the thought of being separated from my friends. "We'll sit on the bottom two," I said as I moved through the crowded aisle.

Aiden followed closely behind me. We sat and our hands brushed when we both reached for the same arm rest. I giggled with embarrassment and moved to the opposite rest instead. I breathed deeply, trying to relax myself before the theater went dark. I moved my eyes slightly, trying to get a sideways glance at Aiden. His chiseled face looked stormy and dangerous from the side, kind of how his eyes did from the front. I studied him. He seemed to sense me because he turned to me. His eyes locked on mine, seemingly putting me into a trance, and my hand moved toward his. Just before I gripped his fingers, J cleared her throat behind me.

My thoughts seemed to clear like fog lifting from the ground—a fog I hadn't even realized I was sinking into until now. I turned slowly. My mind and body were not my own anymore. I looked at J. My eyes stared deeply into hers but everything still felt disconnected. I was screaming inside. I was trapped in my own body.

"Liv?"

The voice coming from mouth didn't seem like my own. It sounded distant and foreign. "Yeah?"

She gripped me tightly and shook me. "Liv, what's wrong?"

I glanced back at Aiden, who still looked like a wild storm brewing, and I shrugged in confusion.

"Olivia, you ok?" I could hear Mark asking.

"I think we need to go," I said quietly.

Aiden still sat there staring at me.

"I don't feel well, J. Can we go?" I mumbled, forcing the words from my lips.

"Yes!" she exclaimed and stood up.

I studied Aiden's face, but I couldn't tell what he was thinking. My body was weak as I rose unsteadily. I swayed a bit and a strong hand grabbed me. Aiden looked up with a smirk on his face. He was gripping my side.

"I'm sorry, maybe we can hang out another time," I said.

He nodded and let go. I saw J and Mark looking worried at the end of my aisle. I stumbled my way to them. My mind cleared more, the further I got from Aiden. Mark grabbed me, holding me upright as he ushered me from the darkening theater.

SCOTT

Sebastian wanting to go anywhere with me was strange. The rest of my family had been spacy ever since I informed them about the CC, but Sebastian hadn't seemed to care. But he rarely seemed to care about much. I was surprised he hadn't wormed his way out of our family night. The car ride to the little convenience store on the corner was not pleasant. Sadie sat between us, because Sebastian and I couldn't get along. I pulled into the parking lot and stopped the truck. "We're here, guys," I said trying to break the awkwardness.

"Let's get our stuff. I'm hungry," Sadie exclaimed and gave me a push.

I hopped out of the truck with Sadie following suit. I glanced over and Sebastian was still in his seat. "Are you coming?"

"Nope. I only wanted to ride in the car," he said without looking up from his phone.

"Ok."

I looked at Sadie and raised my eyebrows, but she shrugged. I slammed the door behind me. We hurried through the store, grabbing peppers, onions, and tomatoes. The trip took less than five minutes. While standing in line, I couldn't hold my tongue any longer.

"Sadie...he's up to something."

"We don't know that, Scottie."

"Sadie...come on."

Sighing, she pursed her lips together. "We don't know anything for sure, Scottie. Maybe he's trying to be a part of us now," she stated with a touch of hope in her voice.

"Perhaps, little sis. Perhaps," I said, pulling her under my arm for a light hug.

"Oh, crap," she said and pulled away. She was looking out the front window.

I turned around to watch what was happening. Outside my truck stood Sebastian. He leaned against the door, his leg bent and smearing dirt on it. There was a couple in their thirties a few cars away, loading groceries. Every time they picked up a bag, it slammed to the ground. This happened three times before Sadie threw the peppers in my arms and made her way out the door. She sauntered up to Sebastian with fire in her eyes and grabbed his face. She was trying to make him lose his concentration so the spell would be broken. Sadie was a spitfire, her temper fierce when roused.

104

She grabbed his arm and dragged him away from the scene, seemingly ripping him up one side and down the other about his actions. Before I could see anything else, it was my turn at the register. I paid for my purchase and hurried to the truck. The couple had finally gotten their things in their car, but they kept looking around in confusion. Sadie had Sebastian in the seat, her arms crossed and eyes squinted as she exhaled deeply.

She was enraged.

I shook my head in disbelief at my brother doing something so stupid in public. Jerking the door open, I threw my body into the driver's seat, dropping the bag in the floorboard. "What was that, Sebastian?" I yelled in frustration.

He shrugged, and a look of boredom covered his face.

"Sebastian, seriously, what is wrong with you? Sorcerers could have been exposed just now." Sadie said. "And why were you torturing those poor people? What did they do to you?"

"I was bored. So I thought I'd have some fun."

"Fun? You call that fun?" I questioned and threw my hands up in defeat. Talking to Sebastian was pointless.

Sadie simply shook her head. Her hands clenched into fists over and over again. "Let's just go home," she said with a look at Sebastian that spoke volumes about what she was feeling.

"Yes, let's go home to our lovely family dinner," he said in a mocking voice.

It took all I had to not throw him out of my truck right there in the parking lot, but I controlled my anger and drove back to Grandma's house fuming inside the whole way. Better to have Sebastian antagonizing us than to leave him for the rest of the population to deal with.

OLIVIA

My senses were heightened; smells were stronger, sounds were louder, and everything looked sharper. I had no idea what was happening to me. As soon as I got in the car with J and Mark last night, my mind had seemed less foggy, but...everything was startling me. I heard the gears in the engine moving, the grooves on the spinning tires, and my own heart beating. Loudly. J had been really worried and wanted to come home with me, but I insisted she and Mark go and have fun. I had ruined their almost date.

Aiden smirking at me as I left last night was still on my mind. It disturbed me that he seemed to think my confusion was entertaining. He hadn't contacted me to see if I was all right, either. I turned in my bed and propped my chin on the pillow. I drummed my fingers on the blanket and tried to figure out why I felt so...odd. Like I should be angry with Aiden for some reason, but I wasn't. He made me crazy and frustrated, and managed to confuse me greatly, but those things didn't warrant my anger. He was just Aiden.

Sighing, I buried my face in the pillow and screamed at the top of my lungs. It was relieving. Rising from the bed, I couldn't help but notice everything I touched was like new to me. The fabric was softer than a lamb. My phone was heavy and smooth under my fingertips. The wool on my blanket was thick and full against my skin.

Everything seemed clearer. It was like my eyes were brand new. Shaking my head, I grabbed my phone to text J that I was doing ok. I knew she was worried. I wasn't ok, though. Things were changing around me, but I wasn't sure why or what exactly was happening. I decided it was time to talk to my parents.

I climbed out of bed, put on my robe, and shuffled to the kitchen. The room was empty, which was surprising for a Saturday morning. I took an orange juice and a granola bar and made my way to the living room. "Mom," I called.

There wasn't an answer.

"Dad," I called louder this time. Still no answer.

I ran up the stairs and knocked on my parents' bedroom door. "Mom? Dad? Are you in there?" I yelled and pounded again.

Frustrated when I didn't get a reply, I ran back down the stairs to look out the window. My father's car was missing from the driveway. They apparently went somewhere and forgot to leave me a note. Anger overtook me, and I kicked the wall with my bare foot. My toes crunched as they hit the now splintered wood. I stared at only my heel showing. I stepped back when I realized it didn't hurt. I wasn't even sore. But the wall...well, there was a small hole in it where my foot smashed through.

I stumbled back and fell into the chair. I was unsure of how long I sat there and stared at the hole, but it felt like eternity.

The White Aura

My arms lay on the rests and my back was slumped near the cushion. I couldn't move from shock. Something was wrong with my body. And my mind. My whole being felt like a stranger to me. Knocking a hole in the wall should have broken some part of my foot, shouldn't it? Yet it didn't even sting.

My phone ringing startled me to the present. I jumped up and ran down the hall to my room and grabbed my phone from the bed. "Hello?"

"Hey, baby, we forgot to leave you a note," my mom said. Her voice sounded crackly, like she had bad service.

"I just noticed, actually," I said shortly.

"Please, don't be mad, darling. We had to meet with some of your father's associates. We won't be home until dinner."

"Ok. It's fine, really. I'll see if Juniper wants to get lunch or something," I said in a fake happy voice.

"Baby, I'm sorry. I know weekends are usually our time to be with each other, but this is a big deal. He really needs to talk to these people."

Yeah, right. Like we ever spent time together. "It's ok. I understand, Mom," I lied through gritted teeth.

"We'll talk later, then. Call us if you need anything," she said and hung up before I could say bye.

Staring at the phone, I just shook my head in disbelief. She could have at least let me say bye. Disgruntled, I threw the phone on the bed and took my computer to the living room. I needed to figure out how to fix the wall before my parents got home. Since I had time to do that now, I settled into the chair googling ways to cover it up.

Eventually I figured out I needed drywall and a patch. Or maybe it was a drywall patch. I didn't know what it meant. My father never taught me how to fix things, so everything I read was like Greek to me. Frustrated, I moved the potted plant in front of it and vowed to play dumb if it ever came up.

Flopping on the couch, I reached for the remote as my hand grazed the stack of magazines from last night. Curiosity got the best of me, and I swatted them out of the way, revealing the notebook. The designs were magical looking and intricate, the lines smooth and flowing as the pen obviously danced across the cover. Each swirl held a story I wanted to hear.

Opening to the first page, I saw information about Kyle. This book was old, as the entries were written when he was just a baby. None of it made sense. What did she mean by binding? Flipping through, I saw more of the same weird sayings, none any more intelligible than the next. After about six pages, it ended and my story began.

"First Birthday: the binding occurred today and little Olivia is now like her brother. It saddens me to know my children will never experience what I have."

I read the line at least ten times, puzzled by what my mother meant. What experiences would we not have? Did she and dad do something to us when we were babies? Is this why they were so distant? Turning the page, I saw I had far more entries than my big brother. I perused them, not understanding anything, and finally landed on the entry I came across which first piqued my interest.

Gently closing it, I placed it back on the table and covered my tracks. Texting J, I asked her to come be with me for a while. Whatever was happening, to me, with my parents, wasn't something I was ready to share. It was terrifying, and seemed more than a little crazy. She understood, she was good like that, and offered to pick me up and take me home with her. Scribbling a note and leaving it on the table, I paced as I waited for her silver car to arrive.

The sleek vehicle pulled up, her little horn making the funniest sound as she honked. I promised myself not to think about the book the rest of the day, declaring a worry free day. J waved frantically from the front seat as I stepped outside, and I inhaled deeply as made my way to her.

No matter what was going on, J was my constant. My rock. I didn't know what I'd do without her.

SCOTT

Sadie and I hadn't told anyone else in our family about Sebastian's antics. It seemed more trouble than it was worth. He just wanted attention, and I wasn't eager to be the one to oblige. My little brother wasn't exactly a bad seed, but his dark side came out to play more than anyone wanted to admit. I hoped it didn't affect him as he grew older.

I was helping Grandma out at the store today. She made a bunch of dresses in the past week, and it was up to me to tag and hang them so they'd be ready for the sales floor. This was my least favorite part of the job, because one wrong move, and I would ruin her hard work. When I'd first started tagging, I'd ruined a few dresses. I'd begged to magically secure them, but she swore it left a mark on the fabric and ruined what she'd done.

She used a machine for tagging, and it constantly got caught in the fabric. It unraveled the neckline the first few times I used it. Grandma had been really upset, and I'd had to figure out how to fix them without making her angrier. Plus, I wasn't allowed to use any sorcery in sewing because the magic sometimes lingered. I secretly thought it was a load of crap and she wanted me to do it the hard way for a reason.

I was a little discouraged while working. I'd been thinking about getting another job now that Sadie was old enough to come help, but I didn't know how to tell Grandma. It wasn't that I didn't like working for her. After so long working here, I just wanted something more interesting.

I was walking toward the front with my arms full when I noticed a movement near the counter. There was a petite girl with curly black hair who looked familiar. She and a tall guy were talking to my grandma. The guy, about seventeen, had an aura. I stopped in my tracks, realizing we were in the presence of another sorcerer. The girl laughed, and it hit me. She was Livvie's best friend. I realized now, I'd seen her when I espied at their school and their sleepover.

I moved slowly and deliberately through the racks, hanging the dresses where they needed to go. I tried my best to hear what they were saying, but only caught bits and pieces.

"...a tux...one to match my dress..."

"...must....size...measure you..."

"...speed delivery...next week..."

I finished the racking and moved to the behind the counter with Grandma. I nodded and smiled politely and shuffled some papers to make myself look busy. I inspected the couple in front of me. Juniper was really pretty and seemed to have a contagious, bubbly personality. She was smiling a lot, but I sensed a tension between her and the sorcerer. He was somber and looked nervous. His eyes kept darting from me to

Grandma. He was unsure of what to do, so I offered him a discreet out.

   "Hey, man, why don't you leave a number where I can text you when the tux arrives. It's an extra service for express delivery," I said, sliding him a piece of paper.

   I gave him a slight eyebrow raise to let him know all was well. Sorcery feuds dated back centuries, and while I never took part in any of it, I worried others might. His yellow and orange aura danced around him, signaling he was one of the good guys. No red. He scratched his name and number on the paper and passed it back.

   I thanked him and took the note to the backroom where I tacked it on the bulletin board. Markus Lowe was a complete stranger, but there was a chance he could help me with the CC. I had to keep it in mind and see if I could make friends with him before his tux arrived. Two sorcerers were better than one, and in our case, we needed a whole team on our side.

OLIVIA

I ended up at Juniper's house for the whole afternoon. Mark had bailed on her after ordering his tux. She was disappointed when she'd picked me up, so I suggested we watch movies or go for a walk to clear our minds. J and Mark had it bad for one another, it was obvious, but this dance they did around each other, skirting around their feelings, was getting old. Tell each other how you feel, already! I felt like shaking them both, screaming it in their faces, but knew it wouldn't be helpful.

Tired of hearing the same story about Mark's text messages, I told J I needed fresh air. Heading out the back door, I lost myself in the woodsy area behind her house. The trees swayed in a rhythm that seemed to speak to me. The birds chirped a familiar tune. I felt like I was an important piece in the puzzle of nature while strolling along the path. I ducked under limbs and stepped over sticks, hurrying through the clump. Just when I could barely see Juniper's backyard, a movement to my left caught my attention.

Five feet away, hidden behind a tree, was a large raccoon. His masked eyes studied me curiously as he sat on his hind legs. He appeared to be a little person. I stopped and watched him. We stood silently, regarding each other with intensity. It wasn't odd to see raccoons around at all hours of the day in Arrow Rock. They seemed to always be out exploring the area, but it was strange for one to be so close to a human and not run. In all encounters I'd had before, they ran from me as fast as their tiny legs would take them. After a few long minutes, he seemed to nod his head and went on his way. I watched him scurry into a thicket.

I sat on the nearest rock. Sharp angles protruded into my skin, but I didn't mind. Something weird was going on with the animals in this town. They all seemed to want to be around me. While I did love animals, now that they were so intent on reciprocating, it was scary.

I got lost in my thoughts and wasted too much time on that rock. Juniper called wondering where I was. She was still worried about me because of the Aiden incident last night. I reluctantly stood and started my journey back to her house. She was waiting for me on the back porch, looking fierce with her hands on her hips and a glare on her face. "You were in the woods the whole time?"

I nodded.

"I thought you were going on a short walk! I was worried," she yelled, waving her hands around in the air.

"I was…I was watching a raccoon."

"A raccoon?"

"I know it sounds crazy, but it was watching me first, so I stopped to share in the staring," I said, trying to play it off as humorous.

She laughed and bopped down the steps to link arms. She led me up the stairs to the house. "You are crazy, Liv. It wasn't watching you. Anyway, I remember something from when I took Mark to Anna's today. I think her grandson was there, and he is c-u-t-e," she said, lifting her eyebrows up and down.

I laughed at her expression and pushed her away. "Stop. Not you, too."

"Oh, come on, Liv. He is seriously hot."

"No. Now, let's talk about something else. Why did Mark bail on you, again?" I hadn't entirely been listening earlier and now felt bad about it.

Her expression turned sour and I could almost see the fumes coming out of her ears. "Something to do with his mom. I think. I wasn't really paying attention."

"Oh, I'm sure you weren't," I accused with a giggle. "If it counts for anything, I still think he likes you, J. Maybe something really did come up." I rested a hand on her shoulder.

She looked at me with the beginnings of tears in her eyes. "What if he doesn't?" she asked quietly.

"Then it's his loss. Now, come on. We need to practice our makeup for the dance next week." I pulled her to her room, dancing and making funny faces to cheer her up along the way. After the pampering and primping got underway, Juniper's mood brightened. We laughed and gossiped the afternoon away. Juniper was a whirlwind of emotions, her moods going up and down without warning sometimes. She felt deeply, her empathy apparent for all around her. As long as I could remember, she'd cared for everyone and cried over everything imaginable. I adored her for it, but at times it was exhausting.

She overanalyzed where I didn't. She wondered about things I wouldn't give a second thought to, like Mark needing to help his mother. This is why I didn't tell her what was happening, or about my dreams. She would read more into it than was there, or perhaps she'd see them exactly for what they were.

The truth can be a hard pill to swallow, and I wasn't sure I was ready for it.

SCOTT

I'd put Markus Lowe's number in my phone before I left work. I wasn't sure what to say, but I knew I had to contact him. I spoke with Grandma after he and Livvie's friend left. She seemed to be as anxious as I was about contacting him. She didn't voice it, but she was extremely worried about the CC.

I sat on my couch with my feet propped on the end table. There were school books strewn around the floor and sorcery books on the coffee table. My phone lay beside them, taunting me. I wanted to call this other sorcerer, but I didn't know how accepting he would be. Clenching my eyes, I drummed my fingers against my forehead. Finally, my heart won the war, and I grabbed my phone. I tapped my foot in anxiety while the line rang. Five rings and still not an answer. After the sixth I was about to hang up when I heard the phone connect.

"Hello?" a male voice said.

"Hello, is this Markus Lowe?" I asked.

"Yes, it is."

"Hey. My name is Scott Tabors. I work at Anna's dress shop..." I said cautiously. Awkward didn't begin to describe how I felt in this moment.

"Oh, yeah, the other sorcerer."

"Yeah, that's me. I wanted to ask if you were from the area. I don't meet many of our kind," I said.

"Yep, I am. And please, my friends call me Mark."

"Ok, I'll call you Mark then. I'm wondering if you have encountered any other sorcerers besides me or my family?" I asked him. Might as well cut right to the chase, right?

He was silent for too long.

"Mark?"

"Dude...I'm not sure how to put this. But...there's this kid at school...he seems to have a red aura."

Groaning, I tried to process what he had told me. We'd seen the same thing.

"The Crimson Calamitous," we said in unison.

We sat in silence. My mind was reeling while I processed the information about another sorcerer coming in contact with this evil. "Does he seem to be after something?" I asked Mark.

"Not really anything in particular. He does seem to have interest in my friend, Olivia, though." His conveyed the worry I felt.

Livvie.

"All right, man. Thanks. I just wanted to call and see if you knew anything about this. I'm not sure if we should be worried or not."

"I know, dude. I am worried, but I'm not sure why. I'll keep in touch if anything suspicious happens."

"Thanks, Mark. Maybe you should keep an eye on your friend. I'd imagine being the interest of the CC wouldn't be a good thing," I suggested. Livvie must be kept safe at all costs.

"I will. I worry for her, but I'll defend her if needed. She's been a good friend to me," he relayed.

Sighing in relief, I said, "All right, thanks, man. I'll call you when we get your tux in."

He chuckled, "Ok. I'll let you know if anything happens. Can't hurt to be in this together. If the legends are true, we'll need a lot of help."

"That's the truth," I mumbled. "Bye."

I disconnected and sat clenching my fists. The CC was definitely planning something in Arrow Rock, and it was up to me to figure out how to save the town. I must protect Livvie.

OLIVIA

Sunday mornings were always the same with my parents. My dad sat at the kitchen table with his left leg in the fourth chair while he read the newspaper. My mother cozied next to him with a cup of coffee in her right hand and a health magazine in the left. They didn't talk. They didn't ask about my week. They didn't ask about school. They did their own thing.

I shuffled my bunny slippers down the hallway from my room to the kitchen. I pushed the door open and made my way to the refrigerator. I glanced back at them to see if they had even noticed my entrance. Nope. Inhaling deeply, I grasped at the cup nearest to me and barely got ahold of it. I poured myself half a glass of juice and walked to the table. They still didn't acknowledge me. "Good morning, parentlings." Sitting the cup in front of me, I waited.

My mother glanced up and smiled. "Good morning, darling." Then she went back to reading her magazine.

The White Aura

I tapped my slippers while contemplating my next move. Striking as quickly as I could, I grabbed her magazine and his newspaper in one swoop.

"Olivia…"

"What are you doing?"

"Listen. I need to talk to both of you. It's serious. Why aren't you ever around anymore?" I asked.

My mother glanced at my father, a silent discussion passing between their eyes. "Dear," my father started, "we told you we were busy with work. That's all. I'm sorry."

"Something is going on. Weird stuff. Do you two know about it?"

My mother's eyes widened, and she looked down quickly. My father cleared his throat and slid his leg back to the linoleum. "No, Olivia. We can't talk about anything that may be happening to you."

My eyes narrowed, and my mouth fell open in shock. "What…?"

"Just…know we are here for you, baby," my mother said in her sweetest voice.

I shook my head in confusion. "No, it doesn't sound like you are, considering you can't talk about it." I air-quoted the words he'd said, spat them back at him. What was wrong with these two? Why were they acting this way?

"We're sorry, but we can't," my father said. He placed both hands on the table.

"You're serious? I tell you weird things are taking place, not even going into detail, and you immediately say we can't talk about it? What kind of parents are you?" I asked.

My mother's eyes welled up with big tears. She reached for my father's hand, and they sat there, not saying a word. Not denying that something was occurring with me. My chair made a loud screeching noise as I slid it back and kicked it before walking away from the table. In my anger, I somehow knocked my juice over and ruined their papers. Not that I cared at this point. I stood at the doorway, with my hands on my hips, and my body shook with anger. "I can't even talk to either of you right now. I don't know what's happening to me. I can't believe you won't help me." I couldn't stop the tears that started falling. I wasn't even given a chance to explain what was going on before being shut down. Mom had no problems asking about my health every other day, but was no help when I actually went to her with a problem.

"We love you," my mother called as I rushed out of the kitchen. Her words echoed around me, a reminder of how alone I truly was.

SCOTT

Between researching the descendants of Devlin Hart—and getting nowhere— and keeping track of the CC, I hardly had time to study for finals. Santos was a lifesaver. He went above and beyond the brotherly role and dove head first into the descendant research for me. I wasn't sure I could wait until October to be with my Livvie. And with Aiden lurking around, our time could run out much faster than expected.

The thought sent shivers down my spine.

The odd thing about this "Aiden" character was how he wasn't hiding the fact that he's a sorcerer. He knew Mark was aware of who he was, yet he still came around. There was something really weird about this evil being. His confidence was unusually high, but it was often the case for especially powerful magical beings. Our only hope was his cocky attitude would give us the key we needed to destroy him.

Lately, I had been researching legends on sorcery. Humans wrote all kinds of fun stories about us they thought were folklore. Most were actually our history, only humanized a little. Grasping at anything I could, I wanted to absorb all information about the CC before I faced him. It could be any moment, any second, really. No one knew his plan, other than his love for Delana that was fueling his quest. Turning to human folklore was probably absurd, but any extra intelligence at this point was welcomed.

There was one in particular about an evil sorcerer. His lover had been murdered, and in his devastation, the loss of his soul mate killed him. The evil sorcerer had a red aura. Humans knew about sorcerers having auras, but couldn't see them, thus hiding our identities. This story was definitely about the CC. Only the humans got it wrong. He hadn't been killed. In fact, he seemed as strong as ever. He sensed me espying easily enough. Between the legends of sorcery and the folklore, I was beginning to think I had his story.

He and Delana fell in love, and the two sorcerers held the world at their fingertips. The darkness in them both ran rampant, and soon it controlled their decisions. One bad choice led to another, and eventually Delana was destroyed for her behavior. The CC, who was never named other than his title, sought revenge. Using every ounce of power he held, he murdered those responsible and then some. He was on a rampage, his grief feeding his power until he'd grown stronger than any other. Centuries had passed, and still he wanted his love back. How losing his mate didn't kill him, I didn't know. Perhaps they weren't true heart mates, or maybe he was powerful enough to counteract it.

Either way, he must be stopped. No matter what his plans for Livvie, I wouldn't allow him to hurt her. Delana might be resurrected someday, but not at my love's sacrifice.

Flipping through, I read the rest of the stories. I wasn't sure how I thought the other human legends would help me, but it was worth a shot to look them up. It was interesting to see our history interpreted. I couldn't burden my family with more stress about the whole situation. Sebastian still wasn't cooperating. Sadie and Santos were my rocks, though. They were helping me and Grandma in amazing ways. Sadie was actually getting ready to help me with a big stressor shortly. I only needed to finish getting the supplies ready while she completed the potions and charms needed.

OLIVIA

The doorbell rang when I was sitting on the couch working on history homework. It was late Sunday afternoon, and my parents were away at dinner, per usual. They hadn't told me to expect anyone, though. Things had been tense since our argument, the three of us tiptoeing around each other. I stayed in my room, and they didn't try to explain anything. I declined their invitation to dinner. I didn't really want to go anywhere with them, because I didn't want to be around them.

I opened the door to a girl close to my age. She had long, dark brown hair, big brown eyes, and she was very petite. She looked familiar, but I couldn't place where I knew her from. "Yes? Can I help you?"

"Yeah, my name is Sadie. You don't know me, but I believe you know my brother. He visits you in your dreams?" Her bluntness was shocking.

Well, this was surprising. "Uh...why don't you come in?"

She sashayed through the door like she owned the place. For someone my age, she exuded a surprising amount of confidence. She was wearing tight jeans with holes in the knees and heels that made her taller than me. A fitted tank top with a vest and at least a dozen necklaces completed the ensemble. Her hair was loose and wavy, making her look like she just stepped off a runway. "Please, come and sit down. Would you like anything, something to drink? We have water, juice, and I think a few soft drinks..."

"No, thank you. I don't have time for small talk. My brother found out some disturbing news today, and I'm here to make sure you stay safe. I have some protection charms to place around your house. Also, I'll put some wards outside, if that's ok with you. No one will be able to see them. Only magical beings will know they are there."

Wow, she sure was bossy. "Uh..sure. Can you tell me what this is about?"

"No. I don't want to scare you or anything. We're just taking precautions."

Scare me? Yeah, she succeeded at that already. "Ok. Go ahead. Is there anything I need to do?"

She handed me a beautiful ring. It was silver with a light pink stone. It was delicate and fit my finger perfectly. "Yes, wear this at all times. It's a personalized protection charm. It will help you if you get into any trouble. It'll activate so we can come to protect you."

Umm...cool. "Ok. That's neat. This ring is beautiful..."

"My brother figured you would like it," she said with a huge smile on her face. The resemblance was evident now that I knew who she was. The same hair color, the same dark

129

eyes, though hers were a tiny bit lighter. Their noses were similar, but their smiles were almost identical, aside from the dimple on her left cheek that he lacked.

Since she was his sister...she could tell me more about him. "Yeah...your brother. I sure would like to know more about him. I'm interested in learning anything I can...like maybe his name?"

She giggled and said, "Nope. I'm under strict orders not tell you anything. He wants to woo you himself." She strutted through the house, inspecting every room as we talked.

Well, it was worth a shot. This guy seemed pretty romantic. "Ooook. I guess I can't argue with that. Well, how about you? Are we allowed to get to know each other?"

"Oh, yeah, I'm Sadie. I'm fifteen, and I'm a better sorcerer than my brothers. I excel at protection charms. It's why I'm here. I don't mean to sound over-confident. It's just the way it is." Her face lit up while she spoke. This chick was smart. I wished I could have confidence like that.

"Well, I only have one sibling and he's not around much, so by default I'm smarter than him, too," I said with a laugh.

"Oh, definitely."

I'd never been a fan of awkward silence, but what else was there to be said? I really wanted her to enlighten me about Mr. Sexy, but that obviously was not going to happen. I glanced at the clock and noticed it was after seven. "Hey, I'm about to cook dinner. Do you want to stay?"

She pondered the question, looking unsure. "You know what? Why not? My brother never said I couldn't hang out with you."

The White Aura

Now that the easy part was accomplished I only needed to trick her into telling me something. "Well, let's go. It's right through here," I said as I led her through our long hallway.

The doors to our spacious kitchen swung open, and I held it so it wouldn't hit her. My father had just remodeled last year, so everything was new and shiny. I went to the refrigerator to see what we could eat. I discovered a pack of chicken breasts and some vegetables. "Is this ok? It's all we have…"

"Sure. It'll be delicious."

We went to work. Against my wishes, she helped me. I had a suspicion she was using magic, because she was a super cook.

"So, where are your parents?" she quizzed.

I shrugged. "They aren't around much."

She stopped messing with the utensils and looked at me. "I'm sorry. That must be rough."

"I guess," I replied. I hated telling anyone about my parents. It was so awkward. I explained how they'd been acting, though. Talking was much easier than I expected and sort of relieving.

She kept quiet throughout my rant, her dark eyes staring into space. There was something she wanted to say but didn't know how. "What is it?" I asked gently.

"My brother can't come see you in your dreams anymore. The Crimson Calamitous knows he's been spying and may harm you if he knows you two are connected."

"The Crimson Calamitous?" Was she serious? "Say that again." I was very confused.

"He's an old legend in the sorcerer world, but S..uh, my brother found out he is real."

"S...does his name start with S?"

"My brother? Yes. Our parents named all of us names starting with S."

How cool was that? "Oh, so how many brothers do you have?"

"Three. Santos, Sebastian, and....my other brother. They're all older than I am."

"Those are really cool names. I don't suppose I get to know your last name?"

"No, bro doesn't want you to be able to find us before the curse is safe."

Oh, yeah. That dang curse. "Oh...right. I forgot about that for a second."

Our dinner was ready to eat. I carried our dishes to the table and tried to arrange it halfway decently. I wanted his sister to like me because I had a feeling they were close. I don't think he would have sent her to me if he didn't have a close connection to her. We sat at the table and ate in silence.

Sadie placed small objects all throughout my house. Some looked like wind chimes and some like pieces of lint. She hid them so my parents wouldn't find them and throw them out. She went outside and was reciting something that sounded like Latin. I watched her intently, but nothing happened.

Nothing that I could see, anyway. She walked slowly all through my front and back yards, repeating the same incantation. Her hands were lifted toward the sky, and she was concentrating so hard that I thought she had forgotten where she was and that I was still here. I couldn't help but wonder what it would be like to have magical powers. To be able to protect someone the way she was. It was amazing to me. She walked up, looking tired and worn. "Are you ok?"

"Yes. Using a lot of magic is tiring. I gotta go now," she said, resting against the porch.

"Ok. It was nice to meet you and I hope we see each other again soon." I hugged her.

She felt like a friend, even though we had only known each other for about three hours.

"Oh, definitely. I will be the go-between during this mess," she said with a grin. She looked pleased that she was the one chosen to help.

I wanted to give her a message for Mr. Sexy, but I wasn't sure what to say. "Can you...I mean...just...can you tell Mr. Sexy that I'll miss our dreams?"

"Mr. Sexy?" she said with a snort, "you call my brother Mr. Sexy?"

Oopsy. "Uhh...yeah, sometimes. I mean, he is."

"Oh, man, I'll have to tease him about this," she said with a chuckle, "but yes, I'll tell him you'll miss him."

We hugged again, and she closed her eyes and disappeared. Wow, that was cool. Why couldn't I be special? I headed back inside to finish my homework, locking the door behind me. There was a danger lurking and while my new sorcerer friends, who were most definitely real, promised to protect me, it was still worrisome to know someone was out there.

SCOTT

Sadie was the only one I could trust with Livvie. She would be able to talk to her and not slip up on anything, plus she had more personality than Santos, was more outgoing, and I knew Livvie would respond to her. I didn't want Livvie to know that Aiden was the danger to her. It would scare her too much, and I didn't need to worry about her slipping up among everything else. Who knew? He could find out she knew and kill her then and there. I shuddered at the thought of it when I felt a whoosh of wind. Suddenly, Sadie was standing in front of me.

"Well hello....Mr. Sexy," she said with a snort.

Oh, great. Livvie had let her nickname for me slip. "Hey, I am sexy, little sis," I teased.

"That is so gross. I can't believe she calls you that." Her mouth curled up in disgust.

"Yeah, yeah. Did you get everything put in position?"

She nodded. "Yep, now I'm out of here. Livvie is cool, though. I think I'll like having her around." And she was gone to do whatever it was she did in her free time. Sadie was blunt and focused, rarely getting distracted when she had a goal. It was surprising coming from a fifteen year old, but she'd been that way since she was a young child, I adored her for it.

Gathering my thoughts, I looked at my notes. I'd been outlining descendant information while she was gone. I needed to keep busy because it killed me that she was with my Livvie when I couldn't be. A board of connections made of thumbtacks and string hanging on my wall showed my effort. I wasn't any closer to finding the descendant now than I was two hours ago.

I sighed as I slouched in the chair. I didn't know what I would do now that I couldn't go see Livvie in her dreams. Espying her was still allowed, but it wasn't the same. I wouldn't be able to touch her and feel her presence. Or her kiss. I ran my hand through my hair and tapped my foot. How would I be able to do this for the next five and a half months? I leaned back in the chair and let my head fall to the side. Sighing heavily, I punched the arm of the chair three times.

"Yo, Scott?" Santos was standing at my door.

"Yeah?" I barely glanced at him.

"I just wanted to check on you..."

"I'm fine, dude. I'm just worried about Livvie."

"I know, man. Let me know if there's anything I can do," he said as he walked into the room. "I wanted to tell you that I've been doing a lot of research today. Devlin Hart was a very secretive person...I really hope we can figure this out, though. I mean, it would help our whole family if we could get rid of this curse."

136

"Oh, yeah. It would be awesome. I will help you look more after I get this whole Crimson Calamitous thing settled. There's a chart but I haven't gotten anywhere yet," I said and nodded to the board leaned against the wall.

"No worries. I know we have a bad situation on our hands," he said and turned to leave.

"Thanks, Santos," I called as he walked back out the door leading to the house.

Santos and Sebastian may be identical twins, but they couldn't be more different. Santos was caring and worried about others, while Sebastian worried only about himself. They were my brothers, though, and I loved them. I just wished Sebastian could be as caring. Sometimes I thought he was jealous. He's the oldest of the twins, and he would have gotten all my powers if I hadn't been the firstborn. I shook my head, trying to clear my thoughts. Worrying about my brother would have to wait. Sitting back, I decided to espy Livvie. My relaxation began.

OLIVIA

It was almost time for bed, and I dreaded it. I had dreamed with my sorcerer for a year and two months straight. What would happen tonight? I didn't think I would be able to sleep as well. My phone chimed as I was sitting in the window seat, but I didn't really want to get up to find out who it was. I continued to stare out the window, glancing from the moon down to the trees. That's when I noticed something was moving where it shouldn't be. My heartbeat got faster and it was difficult to breathe. My hands became sweaty, and I gripped the seat, trying not to get up and run. Someone was in a tree watching me—I could see a leg dangling. Our backyard led into a large thicket of trees separating us from the neighbor, and the closest tree, about ten yards from the back door, held whomever this was. I tried not to show my panic, because I didn't want the person to know I was aware. I looked back up at the moon, not letting the shadowy form out of my peripheral vision.

The White Aura

I slowly rose and went to my dresser to answer my phone. It was Aiden, and he wanted to see me tonight. I laughed to myself while glancing at the clock. It was past 10 p.m. There was no way my parents would let him come over this late, especially on a school night. I texted him back and told him I would just see him tomorrow.

Aiden could be cocky, but the past few days had been fun. He was showing me a different side of him, and it was kind of nice. I didn't think I was in love with him or anything, obviously, since I felt something for my dream man with no name. I was going to the dance, but maybe it wouldn't be awkward with Aiden there. I had decided I would dance with him, but I was going solo. He hadn't taken it very well and was trying even harder to be charming.

I went back to the window, searching for someone still out there. I couldn't see any movements in the trees, but I saw the deer from my dream staring up at me. Her eyes were wide and caring while peeping up at me in the moonlight. My mind raced as I moved closer to the window. My hand reached up as if touching the window would somehow bring me closer to her. Our gazes connected, a silent conversation playing as her presence reassured me I was safe and she'd keep me that way.

Suddenly, I heard something behind me. I closed my ruffled curtains and turned quickly. There was a small antique key on my bed. I turned my head in confusion and noticed there was a note: "Tell it where you need to go and it will take you. —Sadie."

Well, this couldn't be good. Maybe whoever was watching me was that red calamari person she told me about. I turned it over to see if there was anything on the back. There wasn't. Why couldn't she have told me more about what was going on? Was I supposed to keep this with me all the time in case something bad happened?

Sighing, I snagged it off the bed and took it to my top dresser drawer. My parents were observant when they came in my room, and I didn't want them asking any questions. I could imagine my response. "Uhh…well I have dreams about this attractive guy, who just happens to be a sorcerer. His sister sent it to me because there is an evil, red calamari after me." Yeah…that would go over swell.

I trudged down the hall toward the bathroom. My mother called from the living room to ask if I was going to bed. After a quick "yes," I slid into the bathroom to brush my teeth. After, I hurried back to my bedroom and stripped. I usually slept in just a cami and boy shorts, but tonight I chose to sleep in a T-shirt and shorts. I didn't feel comfortable after seeing someone outside my window, even though the curtains were closed. I turned off the light and crawled into bed, sad and wondering what the night would bring.

SCOTT

I had been espying Livvie when she saw someone in her trees. It was the CC; his red aura was glowing in the night, the red stark against the blackened sky. I had panicked and sent the key, but signed Sadie's name. I didn't want her to feel like I was invading her privacy, even though I kind of did every day, but she knew Sadie had placed things around her room and home to help keep her safe.

Aiden was getting a little too comfortable. The fact that he was watching her so closely when he knew he would see her tomorrow was terrifying. I thought I knew what his plan was, but now I was wondering if maybe he intended to do this before the dance. Originally, I thought the event was his target date. It only gave me a week to figure out a plan, but now I wasn't so sure. Did he want more than a sacrifice? Was he feeling something for Livvie?

I found out some useful information when researching some of our history books, not human folklore. It seemed he was almost destroyed once before. The year was 1825, and it was right after he attacked the council in England. One of the sorcerers was a dream walker like me, and she entered his mind to destroy him from the inside out. It was the closest to destruction the CC had come in his existence. There was no record of what spell had been used, however. I thought if Grandma and I worked together, we could figure out what spells would work in dreams. Maybe even find a way to take potions in with me.

I wouldn't be able to espy him anymore, but maybe he would give something away while I was espying Livvie. Which reminded me, I wanted to look in on her tonight while she slept to make sure she was ok. I sat back and relaxed, concentrating on her beautiful face.

My spirit was floating. I could see her below me, looking peaceful as she slept. The room was pitch black except for a soft glow from the moon. Suddenly, her face distorted, and she looked terrified. She rapidly tossed and turned with sweat beginning to pop up on her forehead. She caught hold of the blankets and sat up, gasping for breath. She ran her delicate hand through her damp hair and clutched her chest, like she was afraid her heart would fly out. My own chest tightened, because I wanted to hold and comfort her. If only I could. I reached out, knowing she wouldn't be able to feel my touch and slowly ran my hand along her face.

She calmed a bit. She seemed to sense I was near. Then...she whispered, "Mr. Sexy? Are you here?"

My heart almost stopped. How....there was no way she would be able to detect my presence. She was human and humans couldn't observe us.

"I may be crazy and just talking to myself, but I feel like you just touched my face."

The White Aura

My heart did stop this time. I slowly reached out and touched her face again, my thumb tracing circles around her chin. She gasped and reached her hand to mine. She was touching her face, but at the same time, I could feel her.

"I know you're here, and I know you will keep me safe. I've messed up so bad. Leading on Aiden unintentionally, saying I might go to the dance when I couldn't stop thinking of you...I don't like Aiden. I just wanted a date to the dance, and now I've made a mess of things. I'm not going with him. I wish I were going with you." She dropped her hand and lay back. I sat and watched her for a long time, making sure she wasn't invaded with more nightmares. Peaceful slumber took her body, and I eventually drifted my spirit back to my own.

OLIVIA

I hadn't slept well at all last night. My mystery man had become such a part of me from dreaming with him every night that not having him was difficult. I felt like a drug addict, and now I was having withdrawals.

I don't know what happened, but I had an awful dream. Aiden was there. It was at the dance, and he had become this evil, distorted person. Terrible things happened, including death and destruction. There were fires and explosions. I was horrified as I was trapped in my mind.

Even without my nightmares, I wasn't into Aiden, even though I originally hinted I would go with him. It seemed like a bad decision, because now it was clear he was the type to not take no for an answer. Goosebumps covered my arms as I recalled the horror of my dream. I wrapped the blanket around me tighter and decided I didn't want to go to school today. I didn't know what exactly was happening, but I didn't feel right.

I trudged up the stairs to my parents' room, my legs not wanting to walk because they were so weak. I knocked. My mother called out, "One second." I could hear her fumbling around in the room. Odd—she usually said come in immediately. She looked pale when she opened the door. Perhaps she was sick too.

"Momma, I don't feel very well today. Can I stay home from school?"

Her hand went to my forehead, checking for a fever. "Oh, dear, you are burning up. No school indeed. Go back to bed, and I'll be in shortly with some medication."

I insisted my mother and father go to work. Mom was unsure, but she finally caved and left with instructions to call if I needed anything.

The fever must have risen. I was in and out of delirium the rest of the day. I kept seeing Mr. Sexy and Aiden fighting. I was having strange cravings for something sweet and salty, though I couldn't pinpoint what, and I kept having these hallucinations where I saw myself...with some kind of powers. All this sorcerer stuff was obviously stuck in my mind and my fever was creating new scenarios.

That was the strangest part. I had the ability to touch someone and see their whole life. Past, present, and future. The fever must have been really high, because my mind was going crazy with images I never imagined happening, involving people I knew and loved. A battle, or war, was raging in my mind and I was too weak to fight. I briefly remember Juniper calling to check on me, but I couldn't recall what was said.

I sensed a sorcerer there. I croaked out, "Mr. Sexy, what is wrong with me?" Of course he couldn't answer, but the question was meant more for the universe anyway. I could feel his spirit lying beside me, his hand caressing my face and checking my fever. My whole body felt like it was on fire, and I threw the blanket off.

I didn't know how, but I knew when he was with me. The air was thicker and warmer where he was. I wasn't sure if his spirit could even get warm, but that's the best way I knew to explain it. It was like I could also feel his love radiating. The thickness and warmth of the air was nothing compared to the pure joy I felt when I looked in the direction of his spirit. The main question I had was why in the world could I sense him? And why didn't I before? It had only been the last two days that I felt him, but he told me that he was around a lot of the time. Maybe there was something wrong with me. I wrapped the blanket back around me, because now I was freezing. Suddenly, I knew someone was in the room. I knew it was Sadie before I looked. "Hey, Sadie."

"Olivia? How did you know it was me? How did you know I was here?" Her voice wavered as she turned to me.

"I dunno. I'm super sick, Sadie. Am I dying?"

"I sure as heck hope not! I'm here because my brother is freaking out, and I have to calm him down," she said, sitting beside me and lifting the back of her hand to my forehead. "Gosh, you're hot, Liv."

Freaking out? Oh, great. Was something wrong with him, too? I tried to sit up but got so dizzy that I just fell back on the bed. "What's wrong with him? His spirit was just here. I felt his presence."

"You felt his presence?" She looked a little more than panicked.

"Yeah...is that bad?" Getting up, she paced the floor with a worried look on her face. What was going on? Her hands were fidgety and she kept biting her lip. She finally pulled out her phone and texted someone. My guess was my dream man. "Sadie?"

"I have to go. I just wanted to make sure you were ok. Rest and we hope you feel better soon."

Then she was gone, just like that. She was getting really annoying leaving abruptly. I was jealous of her abilities, though. She didn't even give me a chance to reply or say bye before disappearing.

SCOTT

Something was very wrong. Strange occurrences were happening with Livvie, worrying me to the point of exhaustion. I sent Sadie to check on Olivia because I was convinced she was dying. I thought the CC had poisoned or cursed her. Then Sadie came back with some information I wasn't expecting.

She popped into our parent's kitchen, with an angry look on her face. "Why didn't you tell me Olivia had powers?" she asked, slamming her hand on the counter.

What in the world was she talking about now? "What? She's human. How could she have powers? Come on, Sadie."

"I don't know, but I can see her aura now. And I've never seen one like that. I don't know what it is. She's not a sorcerer is all I know." She ran her hand through her long locks, desperation and confusion clouding her face.

The White Aura

Oh, crap. Sadie could see Livvie's aura. A sorcerer couldn't see someone's aura unless the person was a supernatural being.

"Oh, and she said she sensed your presence. What is going on?"

"She told you that? She's talked to me the past two days when I espied her. She never noticed me around before, so I don't know what's happened. Sadie, I think the CC has done something terrible to her," I admitted, stuffing my hands deep in my pocket.

"Maybe so, but I definitely think something unnatural is happening. I can only guess what. I think you need to call Grandma."

Before I could agree, she vanished. She really wasn't one to stick around for longer conversations. It was weird to me, because when I found out I was getting a sister, I thought she would want to talk all the time. Not Sadie. She talked very little. She was always blunt and to the point. It was nice, though. I never wondered what she was really thinking or needed to pull information out of her. And she was usually right. I definitely needed to call Grandma. She would know what to do.

Grandma insisted I go to her immediately. I decided to pop over, although I didn't particularly like the process. It tended to make me dizzy, possibly because I wasn't that great at it. I arrived in her kitchen, my favorite room in her house. It was warm and comforting, like her. She had a sort of old fashioned kitchen with antique appliances and the gorgeous old oak table where I sat so many times before. I stood for a few minutes catching my breath and allowing my body to

149

adjust. Then I sat at the spot she prepared for me. Muffins and tea were spread out on the table. Grandma always had something sweet around her house, just like the dress shop.

"Hello, little one." She placed her hand on my shoulder in an attempt to comfort me.

"Hey, Grandma. Have you figured out anything?"

"Yes, I think so. I'll have to talk to your sister to be sure, but I have a few theories."

"Why didn't I see her aura, Grandma? I was espying her minutes before Sadie popped in to check on her."

"Well, dear. If she really is your heart mate, and I think she is, then you won't be able to see her aura. Ever."

Wait, what? I just looked at her, letting the confusion speak for me.

"I know. It seems odd, but let me explain. You see, some sorcerers have fallen in love with our enemies and not known it. If they had been able to see their auras, then they probably would have destroyed them and in effect, destroyed themselves. You know how connected heart mates are. It would destroy the sorcerers they were meant for also."

"Are you saying Olivia is an enemy?" I barely choked it out.

"What? No. I'm just explaining why you can't see her aura. I don't know what's going on, but she's some sort of magical being if Sadie can see her aura."

"She can feel my presence when I observe her, too, Grandma."

Her mouth fell open. I knew that would shock her. "Really? Then she's connected to sorcerers, in some way."

In some way was the part that scared me.

"I'll do some more research, ok? We will figure this out, little one." She patted my hand and went to make more tea. We somehow ate all the muffins and drank the tea in the short time we sat there, discussing what we could and could not do about our situation. Glancing at the clock, I realized we had been talking for almost two hours. Time flew when the topic was serious. I took my plate to the sink, needing to do something productive. I must save Livvie from this evil. I didn't know what would happen when he found out she was magical. "Grandma, have you researched the CC any?"

"Yes. I don't know what spells will work from the inside out. I think...you'll need to do something in his dreams that will make him destroy himself. I believe that's the only way."

Destroy himself. Now we were getting somewhere. "All right. Can I borrow a few books?"

She nodded, and I left to go to her library. She owned more books than anyone I knew, including a ton of magical volumes. I walked in and went directly to the far wall. Behind the Shakespeare section, there was a button to release the trap door. Grandma couldn't leave the magical texts out in the open for everyone to see. A lot of human friends came and went because she was a member of the gardening club and a book club.

The trap door opened into a lair of sorts. The inside was covered with shelves. Some held ingredients for potions. One wall was covered with shelves of books full of our history, spells, and myths. In the middle of the room was a long table, holding a few ledgers and some pens. It looked like Grandma had been copying spellbooks. She had been around for so long, the bindings wore out. Every century or so she rewrote the pages. They became smudged or torn, and we couldn't risk losing the information. I'd suggested she print them, but she vowed to do it the old fashioned way. She insisted it was the only true way to do it. Walking over, I dragged a chair with me so I could sit in front of the bookshelves. For the next few hours, I pored over them, searching for an answer.

OLIVIA

The last two days had been pure torture for me. The fever consumed me all of Monday and most of Tuesday. I was in and out of delirium, not knowing what was real and what wasn't. I vaguely remembered speaking to Juniper. Sadie dropped by, but I didn't remember what all happened. My parents had been concerned, but I was still angry with them. I hadn't let them dote on me more than needed. But I had to go back to school. Any student who missed school after Tuesday wouldn't be allowed to go to the dance. I didn't want to miss it, so I had to find enough strength to make it through school the rest of the week.

I still felt weak, but I felt a surprising strength in my muscles, too. Plus I'd had a never ending appetite the past couple of days. I'd told my parents, but their reactions were much like I expected.

"Mom, why am I so hungry?"

"I suppose because you were sick, dear," she said, turning from me.

"I've never been this hungry. I don't even know what I want, and nothing is satisfying," I confessed.

When she shifted her eyes to look at me, I saw a momentarily flash of fear, then the usual bored look returned. "It's just a part of growing up. Growth spurts."

Sighing, I left her alone and went in search of my father. They knew something, I felt it in my heart, and were keeping it from me. Finding him relaxed on the couch, I got his attention and explained how I was feeling. He didn't say a word, just shrugged his shoulders and went back to watching TV.

That was last night, so this morning I ignored them both, not even bothering to ask them for a ride or reply when Mom offered.

I would walk to school today, since it was just about a mile away. Surely the fresh air would do me good after being ill. I hadn't heard from Aiden since Sunday night when I told him he couldn't come see me. Sadie hadn't contacted me anymore either. I only felt Mr. Sexy's presence once yesterday. It seemed everyone was abandoning me, and it wasn't a good feeling.

I walked up to the school's courtyard. There were a few trees and some benches for lunching and lounging. I wasn't feeling very strong after that long walk and decided to sit a few more minutes before heading to my locker. Then something moved behind the tree to my right, and I noticed Aiden hiding there. He was watching me with a scary, creepy look on his face, but he seemed excited about something. I lifted my hand to wave. He turned and walked away without even acknowledging it. I wanted to hurry after him, but the bell was about to ring, so I needed to go inside.

Juniper was waiting for me at my locker with Mark at her side. Hmm, I liked the look of that. Maybe they would finally see they were perfect for each other. She squealed when she saw me and ran toward me, her arms open wide for a hug. As soon as her skin touched mine, it happened. It was almost like an out of body experience, a movie that only I could see. I saw Juniper as a baby, small and cuddly in her mother's arms. I saw her walking, talking, us meeting for the first time, the first day of every school year. Her whole life was passing, including the moment we were in. But then...then I saw her in that gorgeous black gown we had bought on Saturday. Her throat was slit. She was dead.

I gasped and jerked back. Mark was watching me carefully, his gaze not on my face but above my head, then up and down my body. I thought that was an odd way to stare. Juniper's yelling interrupted my thoughts.

"Liv! Are you ok?" she asked, concern lacing each word.

I stared at her, eyes wide, and tried to focus on her. I couldn't speak.

"Liv!" she screamed. She grasped my shoulders, sending the whirlwind of images flashing through my mind once again. I couldn't handle the intensity. My breathing became hard as I gasped and fought to get air. It was too much and everything went black.

I woke up on a hard table in a dimly lit room. A woman, who I assumed was the school nurse, stood in the corner making notes. She was short and round, an older lady probably in her sixties. She looked motherly and kind. I glanced around the room, realizing I'd never been in the nurse's office before. It was small with light pink walls. There was a cabinet in front of me that held bandages and medications. The bed I was on was fairly high off the floor with a soft pillow on the hard surface. I groaned when I tried to sit up.

"Oh, dear, you are awake. Do not try to move just yet. Get your bearings." Her voice was filled with concern.

I nodded ever so slightly and mumbled, "What happened?"

"Well, you fainted. I'm not sure why yet. I have called your parents, and they informed me you were ill and missed school. I think you probably shouldn't have walked here today. You will miss first period, but I think a snack and some juice will make you stronger for second period."

I nodded again. I had fainted and now I remembered why. Hugging Juniper caused a gruesome sight. I saw my best friend bloody and dead. I shuddered at the thought. The kind nurse helped me into a sitting position. It happened again. When she touched me, I saw the nurse lying in a hospital bed, looking very old and small, with needles and tubes coming out of various parts of her body. I jerked my head as she turned to walk to the sink. She brought me a small cup of orange juice and some crackers. I ate and drank slowly, careful not to make myself any dizzier.

"Olivia, you will be fine. After you've eaten, you can go to class. I'd like you to find a ride home from school though, all righty?" She gave me a sweet smile and tried to pat my hand.

I jerked my arm back, shocking her with the quick movement. She looked at me curiously but left the room. I finished my snack and slowly slid off the table, worried about what the day would bring.

I got to lunch without any other spectacular events occurring. I avoided touching anyone, just in case. I got to the cafeteria and selected a sandwich from the line. I went to the table where Juniper and Mark sat with worried looks on their faces. I slid onto the bench and looked at them both expectantly. "What's up, guys?"

"Liv...are you ok?" Juniper asked. "You really worried me earlier." She hadn't seen me since then, as I missed the class we shared in the mornings.

Juniper's face...it crushed me to see her so concerned. "Yeah, the nurse said it was because I walked to school after being sick. Do you think you could take me home?" I asked her, hoping that doing something productive would help her concern lessen.

"Of course. She's probably right. That wasn't your best idea," she said with a chuckle.

I sighed. She was acting like Juniper again, so that meant she was ok with everything and didn't suspect that my fainting had anything to do with her. I glanced at Mark when I noticed he wasn't talking. He was staring at me again. I self-consciously slid my hand on top of my hair, checking to make sure it wasn't sticking out or something, then checked my clothing for spilled food. "Uhh, Mark...is there something wrong with me?"

"No, sorry, I was just lost in thought. I guess you got in my space," he said teasingly.

I could tell he was trying to brush it off, but I didn't buy it. Something very strange was taking place in my world. I looked around the lunch room, expecting Aiden to be rushing to my side any moment. He wasn't here. I saw him momentarily before school, and now he was absent. I tried to not let it concern me, but he acted odd. It shouldn't matter if he was here or talked to me, but I felt an odd draw to him ever since the theater. It wasn't a romantic or loving pull, but I felt the need to watch and make sure he didn't do anything out of the ordinary. "Is Aiden not here?" I asked them, turning back toward them.

"No, he wasn't in last period," Mark said.

"Weird. I saw him this morning. He's been so excited about the dance. He won't be able to go, right?"

"Really? You saw him? It's strange he's not here then. All of my teachers say Wednesday or after absences are a no go. I thought you two were going together." Mark looked confused.

I nodded. It was unusual indeed. I didn't know what to think about anything anymore. "I told him we weren't going as a couple, but we were planning to hang out some while there."

"Maybe something happened," Juniper piped in.

"I don't know...he seemed...happy this morning," I shook my head, saying, "He was hiding behind a tree, though. That was a little peculiar."

Juniper laughed. "Behind a tree?"

Mark stared at me, not even blinking. "That's not normal, Liv. You should be careful..."

The intensity of his look made my heart beat a little faster. He was obviously worried, and that scared me. I nodded and continued to eat. At least I wouldn't have to worry about dealing with him at the dance now.

$\mathcal{SCOTT}$

I knew what had to be done, but I just didn't have any clue how to go about it. I spent hours going over the books I borrowed from Grandma, researching every detail about the mysterious evil sorcerer. Along with a few more hours of talking to her, we finally figured out I needed another fifth generation sorcerer to help me. It was our only hope. We needed an immense amount of power, and only fifth gens could produce it. I already contacted the others in our family, and none could come to Loudon Heights on such short notice.

I hadn't been able to visit Livvie anymore. He was watching her, the same as I had. Too much contact might intrigue him enough to act sooner than he planned. I glanced at the clock and realized I only had a little over two days to concoct a plan. Two days didn't seem like long at all.

Stretching, I got up from the table. I decided a walk would be good for me and set out. I strolled slowly, enjoying the scenery. A family of six was working together mowing and landscaping their yard, while at another house a set of parents were trying to teach their toddler girl how to play softball.

I breathed deeply, making the cool air fill my lungs, allowing the air to circulate through my body, opening my senses to all around me. I smelled a variety of flowers, freshly mown grass, and someone's steaks on a grill, all calming me. I quickened my steps, hoping the relaxation of the day would help me to think of a plan.

I needed to contact Mark. There was a chance he was a fifth generation sorcerer, too. It was a long shot, but it was worth asking. With a quick text, I set up a meeting at the coffee shop where I first saw Livvie. He was already on his way to Loudon Heights to pick up his tux, so this worked out perfectly. I made my way over to 4th, careful to focus on all of my surroundings. I couldn't be too careful with the CC out there--especially if he knew Livvie had an aura now.

I had just stepped in the shop and ordered a large sweet tea when Mark walked in. His eyes were dazed and he looked frazzled. Concerned, I nodded to a booth at the back of the shop. He stumbled back there, like he was in a fog. Purchasing my tea, and a coffee for him, I hurried to the seat across from him. "What happened?"

"Remember the friend I told you Aiden had an interest in?" he asked.

I nodded. He still had no idea Livvie was my heart mate.

"Well, something strange happened with her today. She's been sick, and she came back to school with a white aura. I've never seen anything like it." He paused, struggling to catch his breath and thoughts.

"What do you think she is?" I quietly asked.

"I have no idea, but I think it's why Aiden is interested in her. I mean, she's obviously something special, right? A white aura? I don't know of any beings who possess those. And she's apparently got some abilities, because she hugged her best friend and passed out. Dude, it was crazy. I don't know what happened, but she was really shaken up."

"Is she ok?" I asked.

He nodded. "Seems to be, but something is off."

Livvie fainted today. That meant she was gifted with some sort of energy-draining power. "I have something I should probably tell you," I confessed.

"What's that?" he asked. "I dunno if this day can get any weirder."

"You know how we have heart mates and stuff? Have you met yours?"

He shook his head. "What does this have to do with Olivia and the CC?" he asked genuinely confused.

Sighing, I twisted my keys in my hand. "Olivia is sort of my heart mate."

His face wrinkled in confusion. I could almost see the thoughts going through his head. "You didn't tell me you knew Olivia. Wait...Olivia doesn't even have a boyfriend. She's never mentioned you. How could she be your heart mate?" he asked.

"I saw her walking down the sidewalk. I was sitting in that booth right over there," I said as I pointed to the other end of the shop, "and I knew she was it. I'm my family's current fifth generation sorcerer, and I have the ability to dream walk. It's how I see her."

He nodded while processing what I just told him. I knew what questions were coming next. "Why don't you just meet her? And be with her...is this some sort of weird romance thing? Or is something else going on?"

I laughed and said, "No, no weird romance thing. My family has a curse on it. We can't meet our heart mates before seventeen and six months or they'll die. Why not just eighteen, I don't know, but the sorcerer who placed the curse was very specific. I can't risk Livvie dying. Although with the CC after her, she's still in danger, whether or not I meet her."

"Seventeen and six months?" he asked, perplexed.

Much like I'd been when my family had sprung the curse on me. What a random number the sorcerer chose when placing the curse. "No one knows for sure, but Devlin Hart was pretty angry in general and my great something or another's heart mate was seventeen and a half when he placed it. He wanted him to suffer, and he did, because she died instantly on her eighteenth birthday. They lived that six months knowing what was coming."

Shaking his head, he cast his eyes down. "That's messed up."

"I agree. But what do we do about this Aidon character?

"Yeah, I think he wants her because she's an unknown. I mean...what being has a white aura?" he asked again, looking at me for answers.

"I don't know, but I have to protect her. I just don't know how. I've been reading up on how to defeat him, but I need another fifth generation sorcerer. All of the past fifth gens in my family are too far away or too occupied to come help me."

"I wish I was. My uncle is our family's current fifth gen," Mark admitted as he hit the table with his fist, "But I'll still help you. I care about Olivia, too. I've kind of got a thing for her best friend Juniper."

"Oh, I see. Well, we need an action plan. I've been researching, but I'm not really getting anywhere. I think this dance is going to be where he makes his big move," I told him.

He nodded and sat lost in thought. Neither of us really had any idea how to solve this big problem we had. "I'll talk to my mom. I've told her he's here, but we haven't really discussed any solutions. Maybe she can get ahold of my uncle tonight. Aiden hasn't made any moves yet, but I'll definitely be telling her about Olivia and our suspicions," he said as he got up to leave.

"Ok, man, can you let me know when you find out something?" I asked, and we shook hands.

"Will do. Talk to you later."

After he left, I sat for a long time. I still wasn't sure how I was going to save Livvie and protect her from the curse at the same time. But I had to. Somehow. Now I at least had Mark on my side. He was with Livvie every day. He would be able to keep an eye on her.

OLIVIA

I was seriously freaking out. Seeing my best friend die had been terrifying. My hands hadn't stopped shaking since I'd woken up in the nurse's office. Riding home with Juniper was awkward. She knew something was wrong with me, but there was no way I could tell her. I had to think of some way to keep her safe. She couldn't go to the dance. However, I didn't have a legitimate reason to tell her that. She liked Mark too much. Maybe he could help me. But I would have to tell him all of the strange things that were happening to me. I wasn't ready to share that with anyone yet.

I tried to avoid touching anyone since I'd hugged Juniper. That was difficult in the halls of our school building. I ended up sliding my way through breaks with my back against the wall. I was late for two classes because I hid in the bathroom, but I really didn't want to see anything that horrifying again.

I was sitting on the couch staring into space when my father walked in the room. He was six feet, three inches tall with bulging muscles and dark brown hair. His eyes were the same shade of green as mine. I always felt physically safe when my dad was around, though he didn't seem to worry about my emotional well-being. Though we fought, all I wanted was him to comfort me in this moment. Was it horrible a daughter just wanted her daddy when she felt everything spiraling out of control? Maybe this love/hate relationship was a normal teenager thing.

I hoped he wouldn't be able to notice I had been crying. "Hey, Daddy." I tried to keep my voice steady.

"Hey, baby girl. You ok?"

Uh oh, he knew. I'd known he would sense something was wrong. Even though my parents weren't the greatest at being supportive, they were always observant.

"Just had a bad day at school. Worried about a test. I think I'm still tired from where I was sick, too."

I really hoped he believed me. All of those things were true, so I wasn't technically lying to him. I didn't want to tell him about what happened. He said we couldn't talk about it, right?

I stood up and folded the blanket I was wrapped in. I wanted to hug him so badly, but knew I couldn't risk it. Before I could get away, he scooped me into a bear hug. I waited, my body tense, for an image. Nothing happened. I pulled back slowly, looking up into my father's eyes. Nothing happened to him either. I smiled and let go, hoping he didn't ask about my strange behavior.

"Yeah, the school called saying you fainted. Are you still feeling ill?"

"Yeah, I did. I'm ok now. I think I just got too hot."

He studied me, like he knew I was lying. "Olivia, I know things are…happening, and you're scared. I understand, but you have to trust me when I say talking about anything going on is dangerous and could be a life or death situation."

My heartbeat sped up. "What do you mean, Daddy?" I asked, my voice shaky.

"I really can't talk about it, Olivia. Your mother and I do love you. We're only trying to protect you, and as parents, sometimes we don't know what to do. I hope we're making the right decisions." My huge, strong daddy stood there looking torn as he spoke, his eyes misty as he observed me. "You have to promise to be careful and not tell anyone about these…occurrences."

I nodded. "Ok. I promise."

He wrapped me in another hug before walking up the stairs. What just happened?

I thought maybe I imagined the whole thing. I was running a fever for two days. There was a good possibility I was having hallucinations. Though…the memory of my mother's mysterious notebook briefly ran through my mind, and the actions and words from my father just now confirmed something was happening. I went to the bathroom. A good splash of water would calm me. I turned on the faucet and ran my cold, wet hands all over my face and neck. I glanced into the mirror, and the reflection staring back didn't look like my own. For one thing, my green eyes were brighter than usual. Leaning closer, I saw that wasn't an accurate description either. No, they were actually glowing.

I stumbled back and ran into the towel rack. I silenced my "ow" before I alerted my father to any additional weirdness coming from me. Why would my eyes be glowing? I managed to get to my room, holding on to the wall for support as I stumbled to my bedroom door. I knew I needed to talk to someone, but I didn't know who. Then it hit me. I could talk to Sadie. She was a sorcerer, and she would surely know what was happening to me. I hurried to my dresser, remembering the gift she had sent me on Sunday. I rummaged for the key, still thinking it was a very odd present. Finding it, I read the note still attached. It simply said to tell it where I needed to go. "Take me to Sadie?"

Nothing happened. Maybe I should hold it. I grasped the cold metal in my hands, wrapping both around it completely. "Take me to Sadie."

In an instant, I was in a dimly lit bedroom. The bed was covered in black and purple bedding, and matching curtains covered the window. There was a small dresser serving as a desk for a purple laptop sitting on it. Apparently, Sadie liked purple. Some shelves held small containers of stuff. I couldn't tell what exactly was inside. I heard a shuffle from behind me and turned quickly, falling over some shoes lying on the floor. "Ow!" I cried, though that was seriously cool.

"Olivia...?"

"Sadie! Oh, thank God. I need help," I exclaimed.

"What is it? Is someone after you?" she asked, horror in her eyes. She glanced around me, as if expecting to see someone with or following me.

"No. Something is happening to me, Sadie. I don't know what it is." I was almost crying at this point. The stress of the week was catching up and I was scared.

"Oh. Yeah...uh...Sc...I mean, my brother doesn't want me to talk to you about that." She looked down at her feet. She couldn't even look me in my eyes. I couldn't blame her, I would be embarrassed too.

"Sadie," I cried out, "please?"

She took my hands, making me flinch as I waited for the vision, but nothing came, and she led me to the bed. She stared into my eyes, and her own grew wider when she noticed the glow that had sent me here. "Olivia, I can see you're scared and worried. It will be ok. Please calm down." She put a reassuring hand on my arm, causing me to flinch again. Why wasn't it happening anymore? She gazed at me with warm eyes and a heat radiated throughout my body as she consoled me. I was relaxing.

"I am scared, Sadie. You were the only one I could come to."

She nodded.

"My eyes are glowing. And today...well, today, I hugged my best friend and saw her die. At the dance! But now, here you are touching my hands, and nothing happens. I hugged my father and no vision. Am I losing my mind?"

She started to laugh, but catching my expression stopped her. "No, Olivia, you are not going crazy. Something is occurring to you. I don't know exactly what. We're working on that. My brother found another sorcerer to help him, and they're determined to find out the cause of all of this. That's all I can tell you. As for this...vision...you had, I don't know anything about that." Her voice was strained.

I knew she was telling me the truth. No one knew what was happening to me. I was turning into a freak. "Ok. Thank you for relaxing me, Sadie. You know, you remind me of someone. She always calms me and makes me feel peaceful, too."

Smiling, she said, "Thanks. I get it from my grandmother."

Shuffling my foot across the floor, I closed my eyes and inhaled deeply. I had to know. "Are the visions I'm having really going to happen?"

She bit her lip, eyes filling with sadness and nodded. "I think so."

I stood and fumbled with the key. I felt at ease with Sadie. I could talk to her about what was taking place, and she was my only connection to Mr. Sexy. I nodded. "Well, I guess I'd better get going. I have school tomorrow, and I've been having a hard time sleeping. I miss seeing your brother."

"Don't worry. He should be back in your dreams this weekend."

We hugged, and I simply said "home" and was on my way. I crashed into my bed, exhausted from the day, the week, everything that happened really. I hoped to have a dreamless night, since all of them after Mr. Sexy left were nightmares.

SCOTT

I stood outside Sadie's room and listened while Livvie was here. She had no clue I was so close. It took all of my will to not run in and hold her. It seemed my little Livvie possessed more power than just stealing my heart.

No one I talked to knew what a white aura meant, but I knew it meant a rare ability. The CC would not want her if she wasn't destined to be extremely powerful. I didn't think he would be watching her and so gentle with her if he intended to kill her for his little ritual.

The dance was going to be an issue. She said she saw bad visions of Juniper there. I couldn't tell Mark...he would freak out. I needed him to be able to help me, so now I must figure out how to rescue Juniper and Olivia.

In search of fresh air, I headed out to the back yard. Running down the steps, I stopped when I reached the grass, sighed, and walked around under the moon. I resorted to pacing because I didn't know what else to do. My grandma hadn't been saying much, and Sadie was as rattled as me. The rest of my family...well they were still processing that the most infamous and dangerous sorcerer in history was in our neck of the woods.

It was certain Livvie was destined to be great, but...why had it only just shown up? Magical beings were usually born into it, so the aura was with them from birth. Few humans turned magical, and that only happened when something very big and horrible transformed them. As closely as I'd been watching her, there was no way something that big came about without me knowing.

I sat on the rocks beside my mother's rose garden. Our backyard had been landscaped until it was perfect for her. My father wanted her to walk out and feel like they were in the place he took her for their honeymoon, some little villa in Italy. She loved it out here. Once, when I was little, I had accidently hit a ball into one of the bushes. The reaction was not pretty. Sitting in the garden reminded me a lot of the simpler times in my life, before I knew love and before there was an evil sorcerer to conquer.

I plucked a flower from the middle bush, praying no one would notice. I twirled it around in my hand, concentrating on it for some reason. The dance was the day after tomorrow. Mark and I had sort of thought of a plan, though we weren't sure about a lot of the details. He would place a sleeping spell on Aiden and keep him under, while I went into his dream and figured out a way to make him destroy himself. But thinking about it now...I had my doubts. We definitely needed a more solid idea and an even better execution. I couldn't leave Mark with all the responsibility when I knew Juniper might die. If anything happened to her, he could lose concentration on keeping Aiden asleep, and we'd all be doomed. Frustration overtook me, and I crushed the flower beneath my boot. I needed to detail our fight plan before Friday.

OLIVIA

I was getting dressed when Aiden showed up. As usual, he wouldn't come and knock, only text and honk for my attention. I glanced in the mirror for a last minute check of my outfit: a pencil skirt with tights and a dark green sweater. My hair fell loose with just my bangs pulled up on the sides. I felt like being dressy this morning, though I didn't know why. I picked up my bag and headed to the door while mentally preparing myself to deal with Aiden and his odd behavior. It had been almost a week since I had denied him coming to see me. After his strange actions outside of school yesterday, I wasn't sure how he would act today.

He couldn't keep his eyes off me as I walked up to his car. I climbed in, and he was still gazing, his mouth slightly open. "Aiden?" More stares. This was uncomfortable. "Aiden!"

"Olivia. I'm sorry for gawking, but you…well, you look radiant."

Radiant? What was wrong with him? And he was studying the area above my head like Mark had. Did I have some sort of sign or something that only they could see up there? "Well, thank you. I've worn this before..." I said and looked down at my legs.

"I know, but something has changed about you. You look more beautiful than ever." He smiled and grabbed for my hand. I let him hold it because it was too awkward to pull away. He knew I didn't want to date him. "Thanks," I whispered. "Maybe we should go...?"

Why couldn't he stop gaping? Everyone was acting weird lately.

"Good idea. Let's get this day over with. Tomorrow is the dance. Although you don't want to call it a date, I know it my heart it is indeed a date."

He was way too excited about Friday. My mind drifted to Juniper on the way to school. About how I could keep her from going. Suddenly, a thought occurred to me, and I gasped loudly.

"What is it? Are you ok?" Aiden asked me, sounding concerned.

"I'm fine I just accidently scratched myself," I lied. Aiden had touched me, and I hadn't gotten a vision from him either. Why did it only happen with Juniper and the nurse? Or had I only imagined it? Sadie seemed to believe me, and she witnessed my glowing eyes.

"Oh, well, be more careful, beautiful lady."

Wow, he was laying it on thick. "Why weren't you in school yesterday?" I asked, pulling my hand away. As much as I didn't want to hurt him, I didn't want to lead him on more.

The White Aura

"I just didn't feel like going," he said with a shrug.

"I saw you near that tree," I said and I stared at him.

His face didn't change. He simply looked straight ahead, watching the road.

"And what was up with the movie last week? Why did you think it was funny when I felt sick?" I asked, my voice growing louder.

"Now, Whitehead, that isn't what happened. I thought I was making you nervous. I didn't realize you were sick," he said with a wink.

I slumped back in my seat, not sure if I should believe him or not. "Why don't you ever come to the door and knock? Why do you just text me?" I felt brave and assertive today. I asked every question that came to my mind.

His eyebrows raised, and he clicked his tongue. "My, my, we have a lot of questions today. Is this because I called you radiant?" he asked, skillfully dodging my curiosity yet again.

"I know you're just trying to change the subject. It's fine." I paused, "No, it's not fine. It's pissing me off, actually. I don't know what's up with you, and I don't like the secrets. The way you've been acting strange and different."

"Secrets? Maybe I'm not the one who's different. Maybe it's you, Whitehead."

We pulled into the school parking lot then, and he got out without another word, just leaving me sitting there. I jumped out and stalked past him, ignoring him the rest of the day.

School was uneventful, though I refused to touch Juniper again. She knew something was up. I could tell by the way she looked, but I couldn't tell her why I wasn't getting close to her. I asked her to give me a ride home so I could test my theory in the car. That way no one but Juniper would notice if something weird happened to me. I also planned to tell Juniper what was happening with me. Not talking to anyone about it was suddenly more than I could handle. I had to confide in her.

I waited at J's locker after our last class. I was careful to not touch her or her stuff, because I didn't know exactly what triggered the visions. She wasn't saying much to me. It killed me that I'd hurt her, but what could I say? And in school? While walking to her car, I told her I had to discuss some things with her.

"Ok, Liv, what's the big deal? You've been ignoring me, and it's really hurtful. I don't think I've done anything to upset you."

I cut her off and motioned for her to get in the car, and I slid in the passenger's seat. "Listen, J, some weird stuff has been happening to me. This is going to sound weird, but I need you to touch my hand."

Her eyebrows raised, but did what I asked. Instantly, I was seeing the same images I saw yesterday. I jerked my hand back, gasping for air.

"What is it, Liv?" she said with obvious concern.

"J...I saw a vision when you hugged me the other day. And the same one just now. I saw you when you were a baby, I saw you now, and I saw you," I paused, "die."

Horrified, her mouth fell open, and her breathing became intense. "What? Die? You saw me die? What? How?"

"Um...that's the thing. That's why I've been so freaked out, J...I saw you die in the dress we bought last week."

The White Aura

She gasped loudly and started to softly cry, the fat tears welling but not falling immediately.

"And it was at the dance, I think." I began to cry, too. The tears fell quickly, my nose grew snotty, and I was sure my face was red. I didn't want my best friend to die, especially such a horrible, violent death. "I know it all sounds crazy, J, but I've had a lot of weird stuff happening. And now this. I don't know what's real anymore, and I don't know what to do. I don't even know if the visions are real or accurate or whatever you would call it." I was exhausted from all of this and terrified.

"What do I do?" she asked in a small voice.

I hugged her, ignoring the images flashing before me, and said, "I don't know, but we'll figure it out. I won't let anything happen to you, J. You're like my sister. I can't lose you." And I meant it. One way or another, I would save her.

SCOTT

It was Friday morning, the dreaded day of the dance. The night before, Mark had interrogated his mother and grandfather. Then his mom had showed us some defensive moves in case the fight became physical. Which, honestly, I expected it to be. His grandfather hadn't known anything about a white aura either. It seemed Livvie was a one of a kind magical being. The thought scared me even more. The CC knew she was special. All the more reason to want her.

I headed to my grandma's store to get something nice so I could attend, even though I planned to stay hidden from Livvie. Grandma would know what I should wear, and I wanted to talk to her about everything one last time.

My mind kept drifting as I drove. I should be in pain from not seeing Livvie in so long, almost five days, but I wasn't. I expected the reason was because of her visit to Sadie two nights ago. All a sorcerer needed was to be near his or her heart mate. They didn't have to speak or interact at all, just nearness was enough. I drove along the wooded road, wishing my life was as calm as the nature surrounding the road. The closer I got to Grandma's store, the slower I drove. I pulled into the parking lot, taking note of the emptiness of it all.

Anna's was always busy on the day of an event. There were always at least ten people who waited until the last day to buy their clothing. I went to the door, my hand trying to push it open, but the store was locked. "Grandma," I called out. No one answered. I decided to try the stock entrance. She could be back there for a break. I ran around the building and noticed that door was wide open. "Grandma, where are you?"

"In here, dear," she called softly.

I looked in and saw her sitting on two boxes with two more pushed together serving as a table. A box of charms and liquid spells sat beside her. On the table there was one of the huge books I looked at while at her house the other day. "Grandma? Did you find something?"

"I think so, dear. It seems that our Livvie is a mix of magical beings. I've found something from 950 years ago in these pages. It says that each being has a different outer color. Sorcerers are golden yellow, faeries are purple, vampires are black, and evil beings, of course, are red. We know that the CC is a sorcerer because of all the legends in our written histories. Nothing here says anything about a white aura. It does say that if two different beings made a child, it would produce a different color, though none have been documented."

My Livvie was magical. "I wonder what mix she is...and what about our whole war with vampires? What if she's part vampire?" I asked, panicking when I realized what this could mean.

"Don't worry about it yet, little one. Let's save her life first. We'll worry about all of the other later." She got up and led me to another chair she had made.

I sat, my knees wobbling and my heart aching. She was in a lot of danger. "The dance is in a few hours, Grandma. We still don't have a set plan. I haven't found another fifth generation sorcerer. Remember Mark who ordered a tux here? Well, he's agreed to help us, even though he's not a fifth gen. He's been around Livvie and the CC. We talked and trained with his mother some last night. His grandfather is looking into the white aura, like you are. I figured maybe between the two of you, we could find some answers."

"It's a good idea to have more than one person looking, little one. I could miss something. He could miss something."

I knew she was right. This was dangerous and could potentially be fatal for us all. I decided to tell her about Olivia and Sadie's conversation the other night to see whether she knew anything about what Livvie was going through.

"So...Livvie has visions? This is indeed interesting."

"Why is it important, Grandma? What could she be?"

"Well, obviously, seers can see the future. As can psychics. But it seems as if she is a mixed being, so she's had one of them in her hereditary line at some point, from a sorcerer with the power or an actual seer. Did she speak of anything else that's happened?"

"No, just the premonitions and glowing eyes."

"Yes, I don't know about the glowing eyes. Eyes generally glow when going through the magical change, but she is a bit old for that to be happening. It usually happens before puberty."

This was all too confusing. I needed answers. "Grandma? Are you going to be close to the school tonight? In case Mark or I need anything?"

"Why, of course I am! Sadie is coming with me. We figure you two will need all the help you can get."

All the help we can get. She definitely had that right. As the days went on, I could feel my body getting weaker. I needed our dreams back.

OLIVIA

I was nervous and excited for the dance but more scared than anything. I didn't want to lose Juniper. There was that big chance what I saw wouldn't come true. Was any of this actually happening? Sadie said yes, but I had my doubts. I mean, it didn't happen with everyone I came in contact with. There was a distinct possibility I was losing it.

My classes were a blur. I hadn't been able to talk to Juniper because she was avoiding me at every turn. Every time I mentioned my visions or whatever they were, she tuned out. Lunch would be the time I'd get a real heart to heart with her.

Mark was acting strangely, too. I couldn't tell if it was nerves about going to the dance with Juniper or if it was more. My life was completely upside down lately; I didn't know what to believe or what was real anymore. There was no one I could tell about all of the changes happening to me, and in the midst of it all, my best friend might die. The one person I could always count on to be there for me. The person who knew me better than anyone.

The bell rang, and I sulked all the way to my locker. I didn't even bother with trying to talk to Juniper. I was just going to wait. I opened my locker to collect my books but before I could get it all the way open, a hand stopped the door and slammed it shut. Startled, I glanced up to see Aiden smirking at me. Clutching at my heart, I said, "You scared me, Aiden. You could have said something."

"Sorry about that, beautiful. I didn't mean to scare you."

Beautiful? Why wasn't he calling me Whitehead? I looked away from the intensity of his gaze. "So what's going on?" I asked, rummaging through my books.

"I just wanted to make sure you really didn't want to go with me tonight."

"Aiden…" I started.

He stopped me by moving inches from my face. I thought he was going to kiss me right there in the hallway for everyone to see. "Olivia," he said with his voice low and seductive, "I know what you said. I just wanted to ask again."

I think this was the first time he ever called me Olivia. The way he said it…like it was the most important word in the world, made my heart flutter. His hand reached out, and his thumb caressed my cheek. His eyes studied my face, and then they looked above my head, around my ears, settling on my neck. Why was everyone studying me? "Why are you looking up there like my hair is fascinating, Aiden?" I asked.

Sharply, he looked back into my eyes. His face was lost in a trance, and he seemed to be trying to snap out of it. "What?"

183

"I asked…why are you studying me like that? What do you see?"

"Nothing." He seemed panicked. His usual confidence was erased with darting eyes and twisting hands.

"Aiden. That's not the first time. Why do you keep staring?"

His hand reached out and he played with the ends. Running it over his fingers like you would sand at the beach. "Nothing. Your hair is amazing. It always looks fantastic. It's perfect."

He was acting stranger than he had all week. His eyes had changed, as though there was something there, just below the surface. A need or a hunger that he couldn't contain anymore. It almost scared me. Did he want me? "Thanks," I said breathlessly.

Why did he make me so nervous? I was drawn to him, yet feared his presence. His hand dropped, and he turned, moving away. He looked back briefly and nodded at me. Every time we got close like this, he stopped it. Most days I didn't want him like that, but when he was so close and gazing into my eyes, I lost all train of thought.

He left me flustered. So much so that I almost shut my hand in the locker door. I had to hurry or I would be late for my next class. I turned down the hall and slammed into a guy carrying a box of library books. Instantly, I had a vision of him. They were always the same: infancy, childhood, current, and death. It seemed he would die in a car accident later in life. Stumbling, I reached out to grab a locker or wall for support.

"Hey, are you ok?" the boy asked, reaching for me.

I dodged his touch. "Yeah, I'm fine. Thanks."

The White Aura

He looked at me oddly and picked up his books. I wanted to help, but I couldn't chance touching him again. It not only horrified me to see people die, but seemed to also drain me energy. This was the first time I had accidently touched someone since I told Juniper yesterday. After gaining my composure, I apologized again and avoided contact on my way to the classroom.

$\mathcal{SCOTT}$

Tensions were high. Grandma rarely closed her shop and doing so had set the whole family into a tailspin. Sadie was missing school, even though my parents weren't completely aware of that one. Santos was going, but only because he wasn't the greatest at making potions, so he wasn't really needed.

Sadie and Grandma moved from her shop to her house. They were making potions and charms for a variety of things; sleeping potions to knock a person out for thirty minutes, a charm that would blind someone for sixty seconds, an invisibility charm, a cloaking potion for weapons, and a plethora of other things. An outline of what would work best for a variety of situations was spread on the table, and they'd prepped for everything. They were definitely the planners of the family. I was glad they were so focused and organized. I was a wreck. I couldn't think or walk straight. My nerves were on edge. All I could think about was Livvie being captured or dying tonight. It was more than I could handle.

The White Aura

Grandma suggested I espy Livvie after ten minutes of sitting at her kitchen table drumming my hands like a mad man. She and Sadie exchanged annoyed looks about three times before they ordered me out. I really couldn't blame them, because I was sure I was annoying. I was just so scared I couldn't help myself.

So I went into Grandma's library. It was the only place I could get relaxed enough to do the proper techniques. I sat staring at the wall, thinking of all the outcomes tonight could have, for what seemed like days. Finally, I closed my eyes and thought of Livvie. She was the only person who could calm me at this point. I focused on her smile, the curve of her lips, and how she showed just a small amount of teeth. I imagined her hair and the way it slid over her shoulders, softly swinging with each move of her head. Next, I thought of the softness of her skin. I could only imagine what it felt like in real life, but in spirit form it was pure velvet.

I was feeling the familiar stirring in my soul, I knew my spirit was beginning to detach. I counted down from fifty, relaxing more with each number. Soon, I would see her.

She was in school. She looked upset, sitting across from Juniper in their lunch room. Her face was downcast and her eyes looked teary. Juniper looked angry. I couldn't get too close because Aiden lurked nearby, listening to everything they were saying. I couldn't chance him knowing I was connected to her. He'd already given me signals during other espies that made me believe he sensed me. Olivia's newfound powers allowed her to know when I was around, as well, and I didn't want to distract her.

Livvie reached for Juniper's hand. They sat there, staring at each other with grief stricken looks on their faces. If I had to guess, she confessed all to Juniper. Tears were silently falling from Livvie's eyes, and my heart was breaking. My hand reached out in a lame attempt to comfort her, even though I wasn't close enough to touch her. They stood and Juniper moved around the table to hug Livvie. Their friendship was more like a sibling relationship. Aiden was still silently watching their every move. He reminded me of an animal stalking its prey.

The anger I felt over seeing Aiden sent my spirit flying back to my body. I lay in Grandma's library for a long time, just thinking of how sad Livvie looked. How was she going to cope if something happened to Juniper? I had to make sure nothing harmed either one of them. I didn't think I could handle knowing Livvie was hurting so much and not go to her.

My muscles felt weaker. The longer I was away from Livvie, the slower my body got. Espying her just now wasn't enough, I couldn't get close enough for the effect. It was more difficult to summon my magic. My thoughts weren't as clear as they usually were. The longer I lay there, the more I ached. I really hoped being near her tonight would cure me. I needed my strength to fight the CC.

I heard the door scrape open and looked up to see Grandma staring at me. "Little one, what is it?" she asked, kneeling beside me.

"I feel...weak...I need Livvie."

"How many days has it been?"

"Today is the fourth," I said after pausing to count up the days since she visited Sadie.

"Oh, dear," she said feeling my forehead, "the fever will be setting in soon."

She looked as concerned as I felt. How was I going to protect Livvie, Juniper, and everyone else when I could hardly move? I groaned as I sat up. Rubbing my neck, I tried to stretch my legs. They felt like I had been beaten.

Grandma helped me to my feet. "Come, little one. I will get you something to help make you feel a little better."

"How am I going to do this tonight?"

"You'll be ok once you're within ten feet of Livvie. We just have to keep you strong until then."

I nodded. I knew she would help me somehow. After all, she had experience with heart mate pain. I hadn't until now. And it wasn't fun. It angered me to think of the sorcerer who cast the curse on my family. One spell had affected generations of descendants on that night long ago in 1674. What could have happened to cause someone to do something so lasting and detrimental?

Grandma led me into the kitchen. Sitting at the table, I waited for her to finish concocting her solution. I could smell ginger, and I saw her throw in something like thyme, along with garlic and curry before mixing in the magical elements. The smell of the combination cooking wasn't pleasant, but I trusted she would help me find enough strength. I only needed to make it to the school. Livvie could cure me then.

OLIVIA

Four hours until the dance. I could hardly make myself excited enough to get dressed. Juniper absolutely refused to miss it. She claimed she was in love with Mark, and she had to tell him tonight. If the truth killed her, at least she let it out. I fought with her all day about it to no avail. I had finally gotten her to agree to at least let me keep an eye on her all night. I wasn't sure how I would protect her, but I prayed I could. Aiden was captain of the football team and completely infatuated with me. Surely he was strong enough to protect her if something happened.

Glancing in the mirror, I noticed how tired I looked. My eyes still had a bit of a glow to them, though it wasn't as noticeable with the dark bags shadowing underneath. I sat in my vanity seat, determined to make myself look as radiant as Aiden kept saying I was. I caught him multiple times during school staring at me. He seemed mesmerized.

I couldn't figure out it if it was creepy or flattering.

The White Aura

I picked up the silver brush on my table, gliding it through my wavy auburn locks. I brushed each strand until it was soft as silk. So I wouldn't muss my hair or makeup, I changed out of my T-shirt into one that buttoned. I braided my hair, starting on the right side and wrapped it around to the left shoulder. I tied the braid, leaving wisps of hair around my face. Behind my right ear, I inserted a coral flower I'd found at the beauty supply store. It made me feel elegant. I chose simple pearl earrings and the ring Mr. Sexy gave me for my jewelry.

I rarely spent this long on my appearance. Each step had me closer to the dance, to the unknown, to my best friend's possible death. Slowly I moved around as I completed everything, fighting the urge to cry and scream. Uncertainty wasn't generally this horrifying, but after seeing Juniper's death so vividly, I feared what was to come.

My mind raced with thoughts of tonight. Would Aiden show his good or bad side? Could I save my best friend? Even making simple choices was stressing me out. I looked over the palette of eye shadows, I couldn't help but be overwhelmed about all of the choices I had. Reds, pinks, purples, greens, blues, and browns. I glanced at my shoes, comparing the color to the shades. I chose a medium pink shadow and applied it, then lined my eyes with black and applied two coats of mascara. Satisfied with my face, I went to the closet to look at my dress.

My phone chimed as I crossed the room. It was from Juniper. She was here to get ready with me. After I let her in, we quietly walked to my room. Somber instead of excited, I helped her fix her hair and makeup. This wasn't right at all. We should be happy and thrilled, giggling as we chatted about boys, instead of acting like we were going to a funeral.

I curled her already curly hair in tighter swirls, allowing the colors to weave in and out around her face. We darkened her eyes with a smoky shadow and black liner. With a touch of red lips, she looked amazing.

We had always loved getting dressed up and going places together. This dance was ruining everything because of the vision I had. I tried one last time to talk her out of going. "Please, Juniper. I'm worried about you. I really don't know how I will protect you..."

She cut me off before I could finish my speech. "Liv, I know you're worried. I'm scared as hell myself, but we don't even know if the visions you saw are real. I'm not going to miss this chance with Mark and this gorgeous gown," she said, waving her arms in front of it to emphasize her words, "just because something crazy is going on with you."

Her words hurt, and I threw my hands up in defeat, "Ok. Fine. I'm still worried, but I'll keep my thoughts to myself."

And I did. We got dressed in silence. After we finished, I realized how we pretty we both looked in our gown choices. Juniper was a knockout, and I knew Mark was going to be floored. Glancing at myself in the mirror, I hoped I looked as good as she did. And I wished with all of my heart that my dream man would observe me tonight to catch a glimpse.

SCOTT

My reflection was much calmer than my insides. I was an absolute wreck, worried and scared about any strange events happening tonight at the dance. Wearing black dress pants and a white buttoned shirt, I looked formal enough to blend in if I must go in the building for any reason. Mark and I planned for me to do my part from the outside, so I wouldn't come in contact with Livvie. My pockets were loaded with stunning potion, a black, thick liquid that would completely freeze anyone they were within five feet of. All I had to do was throw it on the ground in front of my victim, and wait for it to work. A knife was in my back pocket, big enough to do damage if needed. I didn't want this fight to become violent, but I was prepared to protect Livvie.

Mark was loaded with similar charms and weapons to guard himself and his date. I'd sent it all to him after school. Grandma and Sadie were equipped with memorized spells; immobilizing spells, memory erasing spells for innocent bystanders, slumber charms, and they'd found a few control spells that may come in handy. Overall, I felt we were well guarded. My stomach had a sinking feeling, telling me the CC was much stronger, and this could all be for nothing.

I loaded the bed of my truck with ropes, rags, and cleaning supplies. None of Grandma's books mentioned how big of a mess we would make if we actually killed the evil one. I climbed into the truck, my hands shaking more by the minute. I wasn't so much scared of the fight as I was of losing Livvie, and that it was too soon to see her face to face. All of these thoughts raced in my brain. The damned curse was ruining my life. When this was all over, I was determined to destroy the descendant of Devlin Hart.

The energy-inducing potion Grandma gave me was wearing off. The familiar ache was returning all over my body, my limbs growing weaker as my muscles lost the will to work. It was coming quicker this time. I tried to shake off the fatigue, but it was too much. I slumped in the seat a little when I started the vehicle.

I drove the twenty minutes to the community center where the dance was being held. It was at least an hour before it started, but I wanted to scope the place out. Grandma's car was parked off on the side of the road on the way, so I knew she and Sadie were ahead of me. We were planning to watch from outside the building, while Mark would actually be inside since he was going with Juniper. I still hadn't told him of Livvie's vision. He would be pissed if he found out I knew, but he had to keep his thoughts straight. I parked about a mile away in the parking lot of an abandoned convenience store and made my way to the building. My legs didn't want to work, and each step was more and more difficult. As drained as I was, using magic to travel was out of the question. I'd only end up hurting myself.

When I finally got there, I looked around and then I let out a bird call we had agreed on as a signal earlier. I heard a response on my right. I crept through the trees and bushes, careful to not mess up my dressy clothing. Sadie was kneeling on the ground, laying out her knives and bottles of potions. There was a ladder leaned against the wall, and I knew Grandma was on the roof. In a hushed voice I asked, "Sadie, is everything ready?"

She nodded without looking up. She stayed concentrated on the task before her.

"What is Grandma doing up there?"

"Attaching mirrors to the tops of the windows. They'll reflect down to let us see what's going on when we come down to the ground."

I was lucky to have these two on my side. Aiden wouldn't know what hit him if these two got ahold of him. Of course, Grandma had experience in situations like these. She would know how to prepare better than Sadie or I would. "Ok...so what are you doing?"

"I'm getting everything lined up and ready, so we can just grab what we need. Is anyone here yet?"

"No. There aren't any cars in the lot, and I parked a mile away. It's still about forty-five minutes before it's supposed to begin."

She nodded and went back organizing.

I walked the perimeter. The center was the size of a small grocery store. There were five windows total, but all were too high to look through. Now I understood Grandma's idea. I peeked in the door, noticing that it was only slightly decorated. There weren't any tables with food or drinks, nor a DJ who should have been there setting up. Strange. There wasn't enough time to contemplate it, though. I had to scope out my hiding spot, so I could be settled before people arrived. I walked back to the rear of the building and climbed the tallest tree, a daunting task in my weakened state. After getting settled on a strong branch, I turned my cell phone off and covered my legs with leaves to make sure nothing gave me away.

OLIVIA

Mark had arrived twenty minutes to 6 p.m. to pick up Juniper. She insisted they take me with them, even though I felt like a third wheel. Again. "I don't want to intrude," I said, twisting my hands in knots.

"You're not intruding. You're my best friend. Pleeeeease come with us," Juniper said while giving me a puppy dog look.

"Yeah, come on. It'll be fun, Liv. Just come with us," Mark chimed in.

"Ok. If you're sure," I reluctantly agreed.

"I am. Now, let your mom get some pictures of me and Mark and then the three of us," Juniper said excitedly.

I hurried as fast as my heels would let me up the stairs, knocking on my mom and dad's office.

"Come in," Mom called softly.

197

Pushing the door open, I stood just inside and smiled when she finally glanced up.

Gasping, she stood. "Olivia, you look beautiful," she said, smiling genuinely, something I hadn't seen in too long. "Your hair is lovely."

"Thanks, Mom," I said awkwardly. "Juniper and Mark are downstairs. She wants to know if you'd come take some pictures of us." I shifted my weight uncomfortably. Things with my parents were so weird lately.

"Of course," she agreed. She pulled me to her, wrapping me in a hug for the first time in days. "Please be safe and know I'm always so proud of you," she whispered, curling a wisp of hair around her finger.

Glancing up, I noticed her eyes seemed to change color, then back to brown in an instant. She grinned again, her teeth sharp and sparkly white before grasping my hand and dragging me down the stairs with her. She oohed and awed over Juniper and Mark before finally rummaging through drawers and locating her camera.

We spent what seemed like forever on pictures. After, we went to eat. Although I insisted they drop me off first, they refused. While we dined, I couldn't help noticing the way Mark looked at Juniper. There was no way he wasn't in love with her. I wanted her to be happy, so I hoped he declared his love in an extravagant way. And soon.

We picked the small diner in Arrow Rock to eat. The place was practically empty as we chose our booth, J and Mark sliding in close to each other. Her giggles were flirtatious and his glances were longing all through dinner. I watched in awkward amazement as they explored this new side to their relationship. Each compliment garnered a blush from J, each outrageous comment earned a wide-eyed, glazed-over look from Mark. The two of them were in their own little world, with me invading, as they picked and nibbled on their meals. Finally, he grabbed her hand, the silence following in the seconds after deafening before she locked her fingers around his and grinned widely.

It was so cute, and I couldn't hide my excitement for her. When finished, we all situated ourselves in the car, Juniper seeming to be the only excited person present. Why wasn't Mark? We were silent, aside from her chattering. When we pulled into the parking lot, I noticed it was empty. I wondered if we were in the right place.

"This is the address they gave us at school," Mark said, confusion in his voice.

"Why isn't anyone here? It's all everyone has talked about for weeks..." I said as I looked around.

"Maybe we should just go in, see what's going on," Juniper said.

Terror rose in my stomach. Something was not right. I didn't how, but I knew this had to do with the vision of Juniper. I felt like I was in a horror movie, and we were the idiots walking right into the room where the killer was. It was possible we truly were the idiots. I didn't know who would want to kill Juniper, but I was afraid this eerie silence and deserted lot were a part of the plot. Dread filled me, bubbling in my stomach, as I realized we had to go in. My best friend was nothing if not stubborn and wouldn't give any of us any other option.

"Ok, Juniper, will you stay right with me? I'm scared of this place," I said, terror truly in my voice. I didn't even have to pretend.

She sighed, "Liv, I know what you're doing. We'll be fine. We have a big strong guy here to protect us," she said, glancing at Mark and giving him a wink. "Now, let's quit being babies and go see what's going on."

I felt restless and the hair on the back of my neck was standing up as we walked to the building. I felt goose bumps popping up all over my arms, but I tried to remain calm. Mark and Juniper walked ahead of me and I noticed an outline of something sticking out of Mark's back pocket. It had the shape of a knife.

Breathing heavier, I tried to get closer without raising suspicions. I wasn't going to be able to find out without actually grabbing it from his pocket, and I couldn't do that. Surely Mark wasn't the one who had killed Juniper in the vision. It didn't make sense. It was obvious he was in love with her.

They walked in the front door, stopping just inside. Not really paying attention, I ran right into Juniper's back, making a squeak at the impact. I looked around, noticing the entire room was empty. There were a few decorations, some streamers on the walls, and balloons tied to a chair in the corner. There was a sign hanging on the wall that said, "ARH Spring Dance," and it had been slashed right through the middle. The chairs had been moved out of the way to make a dance floor, but no music played. No students from school or chaperones were in sight. There was a strange feeling hanging in the air. A darkness loomed overhead, ready to strike at any moment.

A sound behind the stage in the front of the room made us all jump and turn our heads. Aiden was walking slowly and cautiously from around the back with his head cast down. At first my heart raced more, because I thought something was wrong. But then...he looked up. His eyes stared straight into mine and he had a devilish grin on his face. His red, glowing eyes looked at me with a hunger in them.

SCOTT

The CC slashed the banner as soon as he came in. He cast spells near the door. My guess was to make sure Livvie, Mark, and Juniper wouldn't be able to leave. His eyes glowed with anger and hatred. I still didn't know how he made sure no one else showed up, but I really hoped no one was injured or dead. I leaned closer to the building, holding on tighter to the branch, to watch his movements. I didn't see any weapons with him, but I suppose with his powers he wouldn't need any. I watched him move to the back of the stage when they pulled into the lot. The opportunity was perfect to take him down, but with Grandma and Sadie both running back to the car for the forgotten sleeping potion to assist Mark, I was helpless. I couldn't dreamwalk and hold a spell over him to induce slumber simultaneously. I was beginning to think this was a game to him.

Livvie walked in and my heart stopped. I leaned closer and closer, hoping to shorten the distance so I could heal. Warmth began to seep into my core. I was close enough. I stayed in an awkward position long enough for the ache in my legs to subside. My muscles tightened, and I felt stronger. I glanced back inside and studied Livvie.

She looked absolutely stunning in her dress. It was hard for me to keep my eyes off her. Sadie clearly anticipated this happening, because she threw a rock at me to bring me back to the present. I made a mental note to remember to thank her later. When the CC looked at Livvie, I felt a rage in me I had never felt before. His eyes devoured her, and I knew he wanted her to be his mate. He knew she was going to be powerful, and he wanted to take advantage of it. All my suspicions were wrong. He may have originally wanted Delana back, but now...the heat in his gaze revealed his true intentions. My heart beat rapidly as the truth sank in.

I leaned my head closer to the window, trying to hear everything.

"Aiden...what's going on with your eyes...?" Livvie's voice was trembling.

A deep, satanic voice answered her, "My dear Olivia, this is my natural state. I've decided tonight is the night we become forever mates. You...you are a gem in our world. A rare piece of magic I plan to keep all to myself. Together, we can rule the world and everyone in it." He threw his arms up in the air and turned in a circle. An evil smile crossed his face and his eyes ravished Livvie.

"I'm powerful? I'm sorry, Aiden, you have this all wrong. I think you want someone else." She turned to run out, but an invisible force field threw her back into the room, sending her flying and landing on the floor. Now she was even closer to Aiden. Juniper looked terrified, and Mark drew the knife from his back pocket, holding it against his leg so no one would notice.

"No, I want you, and I always get what I want." His laugh was deep and made the walls shake, reminding me of how evil this being truly was.

Livvie looked around, searching to see if there was anyone to help. I wanted to jump down and save her. I longed to destroy the CC once and for all. I fought the urge and stayed where I was, holding my breath when she moved a little closer to him.

"Why do you want me, Aiden? Or is that your real name? Are you the red calamari that I heard about?"

His head turned sharply, his face in a rage, "Red Calamari! What did you dare call me, little girl?" Chairs flew across the room. Livvie jumped back and Mark pushed her behind him. The knife was visible now, and he took the stance of a warrior.

"What are you going to do, little sorcerer boy? Fight me? I don't think so." The CC was taunting him now, his voice mocking and his eyes dancing with laughter. I knew he was trying to get the best of Mark, and I prayed he kept his cool.

"Well, why not? You don't like to fight? I thought the red calamari liked a good fight." Mark mocked back. This wasn't a good move, but I found it humorous.

A chair went flying right at Mark, and he ducked just in time and Livvie and Juniper dropped to the ground. The CC turned his head to the side, a slight grin crossed his lips, and he extended his right arm forward. His hand curved up and closed, and suddenly Livvie was lifted, then pulled across the room, feet dragging across the floor. Her screams were almost too much, and I prepared to make myself known. He stopped her about three feet away from him. Her body was completely stiff and motionless, like he had numbed her. He looked her up and down, a hungry look on his face, and a low growl escaped him. "See? I'll have you, whether you want me to or not. I'm going to release you, but if you run...know your friends will die.'"

She stood frozen, but I could tell when he released her. Her body went tense, and she glanced around. Then, she became brave and stood tall. She stared right into those red eyes, squinting in anger. "I would rather die than be with you. But you won't hurt my friends. You don't want them. You want me," she said through gritted teeth.

Oh, no. She was braver than I thought, and I fell in deeper love. But I knew this wasn't going to end well. I clambered down the tree, knowing I was needed in the front with Mark. I slid past Sadie, looking in her wide eyes. She nodded in understanding and handed me a vial. It was filled with black liquid, I assumed was a blinding charm. I crept along the building, keeping my body flat and my steps silent. At the front door, I slipped inside, and Mark straightened. He heard me. I crossed to stand beside him and saw a sight I wasn't prepared for. The CC held Livvie as his hostage, his fists in her hair and a knife at her throat.

OLIVIA

I hadn't expected Aiden to capture me and try to slice my neck. I looked around wildly and shock overtook my body when I realized Mr. Sexy was standing beside Mark. He was here. He came to save me. And damn, he was even hotter in person. His hair was ruffled, like he had just crawled out of bed, and he was in formal attire. Black pants and a white buttoned shirt with the sleeves rolled up, showing off his toned forearms. He held a smaller knife than the one Mark had. His eyes locked with mine and a bolt of electricity shot through my body. I fought Aiden, but the knife felt sharper against my skin.

My breathing became heavier, and that's when my mystery man spoke to him. "Let her go. She doesn't even know her destiny. How can you kill her if you want her so badly?"

My destiny? What in the world was he talking about?

"Shut up, Tabors. Yeah, I know who you are. I knew you were watching me, so I researched you. I know all about your family...and your little *crush* on Olivia," Aiden said with a laugh.

"Don't mock me, *Aiden*. I know a bit about you, too. Why do you want Olivia? I thought you wanted to find a sacrifice for Delana. Is she too powerful for you, big bad sorcerer? You know you can't kill her, don't you? She's *stronger* than you." My mystery man's words made no sense to me, but his taunting was working and Aiden's grip on my hair was loosened slightly.

Recalling Delana's name, I gasped. That was who Juniper overheard him talking about at school one day. I searched for Juniper and noticed she wasn't there. I knew she couldn't have gotten out, because I tried and I was shocked as an invisible barrier rippled through my body. I peered at Mark, my mind trying to will him to look at me. But his eyes were focused on Aiden, as were Mr. Sexy's. Suddenly, my head jerked back, Aiden's hand tightly gripping and pulling my hair, causing me to cry out in pain. My eyes widened as Aiden's glowing pupils glared into mine. He acted like a rabid animal, his head twitching back and forth. "What do you want?" I pleaded with him.

"You heard me--you know what I want. But first...I have to get rid of lover boy and your friends. I know you'll be upset, but one of these days you'll get over it. If not, I can cast a spell to help you forget them all." He released my head, and I fell to the tile floor, injuring my leg as I landed on it sideways. I cried out, and Juniper ran to my side.

"Where have you been?" I mouthed to her.

"I was sneaking around the back. I think I found a way out," she whispered while her hands checked my leg for breaks. I winced as she pushed on the spot just below my knee.

"I don't think it's broken, but we need to be careful when you walk just in…"

She was cut off. Aiden grabbed her by the hair, just as he had me. He pulled her to her feet, and she let out a painful scream. She looked terrified, and she whimpered for Mark. My heart stopped as I realized what was about to happen. He held her in the same position he had me in. Only this time there was no reason to keep her around. He looked at me, a glimmer of excitement in his eyes, and ever so slowly, slicing the knife across the tender skin on her neck. Hot, red liquid blinded me as her body dropped with a thud, her head falling in my lap. Blood spurted out of her neck, the sweet, salty smell momentarily distracting me as it covered my gown and everything around me. I pressed my hand on the wound, but there was no point. I looked into her hollow eyes and felt my heart being ripped out of my body.

SCOTT

Livvie's scream shook the silence. It burned my ears and pierced my heart. Looking at her, I realized her vision had come true. Juniper lay still and bloodied in her lap, her neck sliced open. Livvie's beautiful white dress was smeared in blood, and her hands were no longer visible. Beside me, Mark realized what happened. A heartbreaking "no!" shot through the air, and he fell to his knees. The knife slid out of his reach, and he doubled over, clutching his stomach. Sadie and Grandma appeared beside me, somehow getting through his wards with their magic. Now, we were all trapped in this building. Grandma looked disgusted, and Sadie threw up in the trash can.

Aiden stood smirking at us with his bloodied knife in hand. He laughed as he studied each of us. Beside me, Mark seemingly found his strength. He jumped to his feet, his teeth bared and his hands reaching out like claws. He flew at Aiden with an amazing force, grabbing his throat and knocking him to the floor. *"You killed her! You killed my heart mate! I'm going to murder you!"* He growled at him through clenched teeth.

More laughs. The CC reveled in the pain he'd caused. He showed no remorse, only glee as he watched Mark lose it.

Sadie ran to Mark's side, chanting some unrecognizable words, and threw a vial of green liquid in Aiden's face. He stopped yelling and moving. She had hit him with the immobility spell, meaning we only had about five minutes to figure out how to save ourselves from Juniper's fate.

I ran to the middle of them, pulling on Mark and saying, "Get up. There's may still be a chance. My grandmother is a healer. We have to do something, or he will kill us all." I handed him my knife, "Stab him a few times, but don't lose your head."

He did as I asked, stabbing the CC twice in the heart. A black liquid oozed from his wounds. It smelled like dead fish and stuck to Mark's fingers. He glanced up, face wet with tears, and stood. Holding the blackened knife, he stared at Juniper's limp body and once again broke down. The knife fell, clattering to the floor, and he rushed to her.

Beside me, Grandma lifted Juniper and took her to the stage at the front of the room. She arranged her so we could work on bringing her back later. I really hoped it would be possible. It wasn't unheard of to bring someone back from the dead, but I'd never seen it done myself.

I searched for Livvie, who had grown quiet after her initial screams. She sat on the floor in shock, only staring at Sadie. Sadie was attempting to heal her leg, but she wasn't powerful enough. I knelt beside them, laying my hand on her knee. Electricity shot through the room, my head spun, and a fire ignited between Livvie and me. She looked up with those green eyes, brighter than usual, and slowly reached her hand out. She caressed my face and softly said, "It's you," before she passed out.

I cradled her in my arms but had to stop short. There wasn't time to move Livvie, because the CC came back to life, and he was even angrier than before. The time for playing around with us was over. He rose to his feet, a roar bellowed from his throat, and the windows shattered. We all moved swiftly. Mark ran to Aiden's back while I slashed at his front. He cocked his head to the side, and I knew he had more up his sleeve. He smirked and challenged me to a sorcerers duel over Livvie, showing how ancient he truly was.

"If you want her, you have to win her," he sneered.

"This is the twenty-first century. You might wanna learn a few things. She's not a possession," I replied.

"Duel me if you want her," he spat, his face red with fury.

Sorcerers would duel over disagreements back in the 1400s but I hadn't read anything about one since I had begun learning of our history. My gut told me there was more to this than he was letting on. "Why should we have to duel? She's my heart mate. I know she is."

"Are you scared, Tabors?"

"Never. Choose your weapon."

"Brawn."

We both bowed, customary in a sorcerer's duel, and faced each other. The opponents were to respect each other and not make any movements not defined under the terms. If anyone cheated, death was guaranteed. It was a sorcerer law. It had been around for centuries, and the council would destroy anyone who cheated. Not that the council was strong enough to defeat this evil. He was still here wasn't he? Since the CC had chosen brawn, we wouldn't be able to use magic in this duel. Only our strength and our wits. I wasn't worried about the wits, but strength may be a problem. This was an ancient sorcerer I was dealing with. And even with his injuries, he was ten times stronger than me.

Sadie snuck up beside me, chanting a few Latin words and dousing my back with a warm liquid. I really hoped she knew what she was doing. I didn't want her to ruin the small chance I had before I even started.

The dance began. We circled each other like wolves snarling over the same prey. My eyes never left his limbs. I knew the second I got distracted, he would attack. I slung myself to the right but at the last instant skidded to the left, leaving him flailing about, trying to keep steady. I took the opportunity to kick him in the rear and knocked him completely down. Outraged, he jumped up and spun around. He slammed into my chest, and I flew back, landing with a loud thud. My chest burned, and my bones ached. I prayed nothing was broken. As a healer, my body would mend itself fairly quickly, but I didn't have the time to wait.

Rising unsteadily to my feet, I circled him again. I wouldn't win this duel. I had to find a way out so we could use our powers. I shifted my eyes to Grandma momentarily, hoping she would have an idea. The only way the duel could end before death was if both parties agreed to discontinue. I knew Aiden wouldn't agree. He knew as well as I that he would win this fight and Livvie. Grandma flung her hands out at him, her mouth moving as she chanted words I couldn't hear. He stopped moving and looked confused. "What did you do to me?"

"Nothing, but I don't think we should fight anymore, do you?"

"Well, of course not...wait...you're trying to get out of this. One of them cast a spell on me. Fine! If you want to use powers, we will."

The spell hadn't been strong enough to last more than a few seconds. The more we fought, the more I realized how strong he was. My heart longed for Livvie to be safe. I wanted her out of this battle, but we were trapped. The pure evil being looked at all of us, amusement radiating from his face. "Are you ready?" he asked with a grin and laugh.

His arms spread wide over his head, and his eyes glowed a fierce red. He shifted and knocked us all off our feet. Stunned, we scrambled to get back up, just to have him knock us down again. His sadistic laugh rang out, and he looked around the room at his hostages. "Are you ready to give up, you stupid sorcerers?"

OLIVIA

I woke up sprawled on the floor. My group of friends and saviors were all lying down. Aiden had awoken and was terrorizing everyone. I tried to gather my thoughts and stop the dizziness. Sitting up, I waited for the room to slow down and assessed the situation.

When my leg was healed, a fire lit inside my stomach. And now...well, now something was changing within me. They kept speaking of my destiny, and suddenly I knew visions weren't the only ability I would have. My inner strength was fighting its way to the top, allowing the magic to stir within. It settled over me like a warm blanket, comforting and secure. Everything clicked and I was ready to trust my power.

We were all on the floor while Aiden played his game with us. My rage over Juniper's cold and bloody murder was almost too much for my body to handle. I knew I was defenseless at this point, and I needed to let the sorcerers handle it. Sadie, their Grandma, who was Anna from the dress shop, and Mark were all assisting the man I knew at that moment I was in love with. I was too busy worrying about what was happening to be shocked about the Anna revelation. I glanced around at our make-shift group. They didn't exactly appear to be warriors, but they looked determined.

They all got to their feet. Aiden was too busy reveling in the fact that he'd thought he'd won the battle to notice. His eyes were closed as his clenched hands shook in triumph. His evil, sadistic cackle echoed through the room, proving he didn't think of anyone as a threat. They circled him, putting their hands below their stomachs like they were cradling birds. They closed their eyes in unison and lifted their faces to the sky. I didn't know what they were doing, but they were mesmerizing. Mark trembled, and a lightning ball appeared in his hands. Sadie was next, hers only a small glowing fog. Anna and mystery man possessed the largest energy in their hands. They summoned theirs together. Heads snapped down, each person's eyes glowed with the power summoned. One by one, each shot the bundle of electricity at Aiden's body. After releasing it, they summoned more. Again and again they bombarded him. He didn't wince until the assault went on for at least twenty minutes. Still, he stood frozen in place like a statue.

I noticed they were all growing tired. Sadie looked as if she might pass out at any moment. I struggled to my feet, closed my eyes, and tried to grab the burning sensation I felt growing in my stomach. It was a fire hot enough to burn Aiden all the way back to where he came from. I imagined my hands reaching in and plucking it out of my body. Peeking down, I didn't see anything. Growling in frustration, I tried again. I concentrated on Juniper, and the anger I felt when I watched her slump in her death. There was a hot spark shooting through my core, like an ember being fed. I thought of how I felt when Aiden threw Mr. Sexy across the room. I felt another shooting spark within me. Looking at my hands at my stomach again, I noticed a small flame. Excited, I closed my eyes to focus on producing more.

Juniper, Mr. Sexy, Sadie, Anna, and even Mark being harmed was more than enough fuel. My hands cradled a circle of fire the size of a soccer ball. Even though it was touching my skin, I felt nothing but a slight warmth. I looked up, a newfound confidence in my soul. "Aiden." I said his name with no emotion. Everyone turned to me, their eyes registering the shock of me holding flames.

"Why, look at you, Whitehead. You finally found your power. I didn't think it was time yet," he said and moved toward me.

"Don't come any closer. You murdered my best friend, harmed the man I'm falling in love with, and my friends. I will make you pay, Aiden." Dream man's face lit up like a candle on a dark stormy night at my confession. His eyes held his secrets. He longed to hold me and love me, but now wasn't the time.

"You can't make me pay, Whitehead. You've just found your powers, and I'm the most powerful being alive. I've killed hundreds. I have more power in my finger than you can even imagine. You have a white aura. We don't even know what you are," he said with that laugh that made my ears want to bleed. "I wanted to sacrifice you, but now I think I'll keep you. See what's to come."

Enraged, I lifted my hands to my chest. I was so angry I felt like I could shoot sparks from my eyes. I pulled the fireball back and shot it toward his heart. He moved out of the way, and it ignited a chair. Screaming, I felt the flames reappear, dancing on my hands. I ran toward him, catching him off guard, and lit up his face with a fistful of flaming rage. He screamed and the black oozing mess started dripping off him. I didn't stop there, though. The rage inside me took over and

Felicia Tatum

I slammed the burning ball into his heart. I was engulfed in power, blocking out the people behind me yelling my name. The energy I was releasing was a part of me; strength and love and anger. Each emotion I felt was stronger than before, fueling the immense power I now felt coursing through me. I was a powerful being, a sorceress of some sort, and I would destroy him. He wouldn't be allowed to hurt those I cared about. My newfound power made me more confident, releasing a strength I didn't know existed.

I lit his whole body into a pyre. He was screaming and pulling at his hair, like he was trying to escape his own skin. His screams died down, and suddenly his body seemed to be evaporating. Then, he disappeared.

SCOTT

Livvie was a fire throwing goddess. We started to wear the CC down with our energy blasts, but it wasn't enough. We were wearing ourselves down, too. Livvie noticed and tapped into her inner power. The power she possessed was unlike any I'd ever seen. She harmed the most evil and powerful sorcerer in history by herself. Grandma was the most powerful sorceress I'd known, until now. Livvie stood where he had been, her eyes wide and her face pale.

Mark and my grandmother ran to Juniper, trying to bring her back. Sadie lay on the floor, exhausted from the overuse of her powers. She was only fifteen, and while she was extremely powerful, she was still coming into them. This was a lot for her, so I left her to rest and walked to Livvie. Each step I took slowly, because I never wanted to forget this moment. "My Livvie," I said as I reached to caress her soft skin.

"My sexy dream man!" she cried and fell into my arms.

It felt good to finally be able to hold her close, to finally feel her heartbeat next to mine. Her hair smelled like burnt vanilla, and her skin was as smooth as silk, though caked with goo and blood. "Please call me Scott, before everyone makes fun of me for the rest of my life," I said with a chuckle.

Her head lifted, a soft look was in her eyes, and she whispered, "Scott." Her hands rested on my chest, her eyes studied every inch of my face.

I couldn't resist the plumpness of her pink lips, and my own moved closer. At their first touch, the electrifying passion from earlier returned, each touch leaving a fiery trail across my skin, her lips igniting the deepest embers of desire. We became lost in the kiss. Her lips moved with mine, and our tongues danced in each other's mouths. My hands found her soft hair, tugging and caressing it. She moaned softly and I remembered where we were. I pulled back, my breathing heavy. "My Livvie," I whispered.

She sighed and laid her head back on my chest.

"Scott, I need you over here. It's going to take more than one healer to bring her back," Grandma shouted at me.

I reluctantly released all but Livvie's hand. We rushed together over to Juniper's limp body. Livvie gasped again, covering her mouth to smother the sob trying to escape. Mark stood beside Grandma, his face white.

"We need everyone to stand back. Healing takes some work, and we need to be able to move around," Grandma told everyone.

Sadie was too weak to help with the healing, so she stood with Mark in an attempt to comfort him. I lifted Juniper's body and placed her in the middle of the floor. I got to my knees on her left, and Grandma got to on her right. We each laid a hand on her stomach and one on each shoulder, near

The White Aura

the wound. I felt the energy surging through my body. My hands felt warm and tingly as I transferred my healing powers to her. Her body took on a yellow glow, and we knew the healing was working. Five more minutes of this and she should be back with us.

OLIVIA

I couldn't control the racing in my heart. This night had been a disaster. Now I stood watching the man from my dreams trying to save my best friend. Juniper's body was limp, the vibrancy of her skin replaced with a dull color, her life gone. She was still beautiful, but now she had an angelic air instead of the energetic liveliness I was so used to. Anna and Scott kept moving their hands along her body, slowly and deliberately. They were deep in concentration, their brows turned down. There was an orange-yellow glow around her body, like she was engulfed by the sun.

I looked at Mark, his face pale and his eyes betraying his deepest fear: that they wouldn't be able to revive Juniper. I wrapped my arms around my body, my nails digging deep into my skin. I couldn't think of that now. I couldn't imagine a life without her. She was my sister.

My mind was pulled out of the deep thoughts with a gasp from Mark. My eyes darted to him and then Juniper. Her eyes were now open, and her wound was closed. Holding my breath, I waited to see what happened next.

No one spoke. Slowly, Scott and Anna lifted their hands. They looked weak. Their eyes were dim, and their shoulders slumped as they stood and backed away. Juniper lay still on the floor, almost motionless. Her fingers moved and her eyes shifted. Her face showed confusion, and she moved in a way that seemed new to her.

My heart raced as I inched closer to her. A hand reached out and stopped me. I turned and realized it was Scott. He looked deathly ill, and all he said was, "Don't. She's got to do this on her own." I stepped back and locked my fingers with his.

Juniper suddenly jerked up, her petite body moving faster than I'd ever seen. Her eyes were wild like an animal's, and there was a hint of red around the rims of her pupils. I wasn't sure what had happened. Juniper was back with me, but she wasn't the same. Her head snapped toward me, startling me. Her skin was clammy, but she no longer looked dead. "What did you do to me?" She glanced at each one of us, her voice laced with fear.

"J...you died. I don't know what they did, but you're back with us now," I choked out through tears.

"I died? Like...I died?"

Scott stepped up, grasping my arm for support. "Yes, you died, Juniper. My grandmother and I brought you back to life. There are a few things we need to explain to you..." he struggled to speak. He was too weak from all the magic use.

Sadie got up from her sitting place. Her face was pink now instead of white. She stepped forward and looked at Juniper.

Felicia Tatum

"Hello, my name is Sadie. I'm Scott's sister and Olivia's friend. What I'm going to tell you may shock you, but it's all true. My brother and my grandmother saved your life, yes, but they also had to do a little extra to make that happen. Aiden, an ancient and powerful sorcerer, slit your throat and you died instantly. There was no healing that. Your spirit probably already had begun to pass over. What my brother and grandma did...they saved you and brought you back as an immortal. You won't have powers like sorcerers or drink blood like vampires, but you will have speed, agility, strength, heightened senses, and the immortal life. You'll never die. Good news is that this boy that's so in love with you." she pointed to Mark, "is a sorcerer, and he will be able to be with you for a very long time."

We all stood in silence so thick I was sure they could hear my heart beating. Juniper was an immortal. She possessed super human powers, though not any like Scott. Or...like me. I saw flashbacks of setting Aiden on fire. Melting his body with my hands. I turned to Scott and Sadie, questions heavy on my mind, when a body hurled into my arms. Juniper was crying and holding me with a fierce tightness. I hugged her back, my own eyes burning with more tears.

"I thought I had lost you, J," I whispered to her. She held me tighter. My ribs felt as if they might snap.

Mark walked up behind her, placing a hand on her slim shoulder. "Juniper? Can we talk?"

Her eyes were shining with desire as she nodded her head. They held hands and walked to the other side of the center, for more privacy I assumed.

I glanced at Scott and asked, "What happened to me, Scott? I threw fire. You spoke of my destiny. What am I?"

He sighed and took my hands. His strong fingers massaged my palms and wrists. My muscles relaxed, and the breath I didn't realize I'd been holding released. "Livvie...I don't know what you are. You have a white aura. You have visions and throw fire. I've searched everywhere for history of white auras and found nothing. I think we need to speak to your parents to find any real answers. All I know is that you are very special to the magical world, or the CC wouldn't have wanted you so badly. You wouldn't have been able to defeat him if you weren't a very powerful being."

A white aura. Special to the magical world. The words jumbled in my mind making me dizzy. Exhausted, I collapsed to a sitting position. My dress was splattered with blood, and my hair was stiff and gooey. I couldn't believe the first meeting with Scott was this disastrous night. My head felt heavy as I placed it into my hands, the tears flowing freely from my tired eyes.

SCOTT

I crouched and wrapped my arms around Livvie while she cried. I knew she was overwhelmed by the events, but I was lost as how to help. I caressed her silky hair, trying to relax her mind. Having her in my arms was tempting and fascinating. I kissed the top of her head and got up to find out what we were doing next.

Juniper and Mark were still seated in the corner, she in his lap and their fingers intertwined. They were gazing at each other lovingly. Sadie was cleaning up. Grandma was the only one not doing something. She was standing in the corner with her arms crossed, watching Livvie sob into her hands. I trudged over to her, my limbs not wanting to move. My whole body ached from overuse and I felt like I could sleep for a week and still be tired. My muscles were tight, my eyes were heavy, and all of my energy had been zapped. I reached out to hug Grandma. Her frail body had more strength than mine, and she held me up.

"What is it, little one? You have your Livvie here...and that's a dress I made," she said, trying to lighten the mood.

I chuckled. "She looks beautiful, Grandma. But...the CC...he's only wounded, isn't he?" I already knew the answer, but I needed to hear it to be certain.

"Yes, little one, Livvie only wounded him. That girl you've fallen in love with...she's something special, Scott. Not many magical beings could harm one so strong when just discovering their powers. She seemed to tap into her anger, and it was released in a physical way," she said, and her hand rubbed my back in circles.

"She has no idea, though, does she? She just got upset and angry and it just happened. Is that why she's crying?" I was desperate to help her. It burned my heart to see her cry.

"I don't know, Scottie...you'll have to ask her about that," she said as she slipped away.

Strength was returning to my legs, and I was able to walk back to her sitting spot without falling. I sat beside her, and reached to hold her. "Livvie...can you tell me what's wrong, baby?" I asked her as gently as I could.

Her red streaked face looked into mine. She sniffled her nose a little, but her tears were under control. "I...I don't know, Scott! I mean, what has happened to me? Is Aiden really gone? Or is he going to come back after me? What does a white aura mean? Have my parents been lying to me all my life?" Her questions bombarded me like hailstones. I reached out to her, sliding her into my lap. We sat, just holding each other for a long time until I could think of something to say.

Finally, the words I needed came to me. "My Livvie, I fell in love with you the first time I saw you, and I had no idea you were magical then. You were only magical in your beauty at that point. I saw no aura. I still don't, actually, because you are my heart mate. You are the woman I'm meant to be with. When a sorcerer meets his or her heart mate, auras and everything else are null and void. We see only the person we love. As for Aiden, he's not dead, but he's seriously wounded. We should be able to find a way to destroy him before he's strong enough to return. I don't know about your parents, Livvie...but I'll go with you when you ask if you'd like."

Her hand squeezed mine, her face turning up to look at me. "I think I love you," she said as she leaned in to kiss me. Her lips were urgent with need this time. She gently bit my bottom lip, making me moan when she stopped. Her eyes shone with the love and lust I felt. Grasping her closer, I growled and she giggled, making my stomach dance with butterflies. "You...you are naughty, Olivia Whitehead. Why don't we see if anyone needs anything else, and then we can go somewhere to get cleaned up," I said, with a longing glance.

"Ok," she said as she bit her lip.

My need grew stronger every time I looked at her.

OLIVIA

Being near Scott caused a stirring in my soul. My head swirled at his scent, my stomach jumping at his touch. Each kiss was pure joy, each gaze a special moment in time. My mind was flooded with the dreams I'd had of him, making me long for his touch. We walked to Juniper and Mark, hand in hand, to see if they needed us for anything. One look at their lit up faces, and I knew they had finally admitted how they felt. I reached for Juniper's hand, my mind still adjusting to the red rim around her dark pupils.

"Come on, J. Let's walk for a second," I said and pulled her up. Her steps were faster, her strides longer, and it was difficult for me to keep up. We stood beside the stage where she had died, my arms covered in goose bumps and my body gave an involuntary shudder. "Tell. Me. Everything." I said to her in my loudest whisper.

Her eyes brightened and a small smile formed on her lips. "Well...he admitted he's in love with me. And he said he wants to spend eternity with me. I know how weird that sounds, but, Liv, I know he means it. I can feel it. I'm so...different now. Like looking at you...every little thing about you looks HD. The green in your eyes, there's even a little glow in them. I can see your skin pores. It's so weird. I can hear everything. There's a dog about a mile down the road, barking and trying to get out of his pen."

"Wow...J...you make it sound cool," I said and playfully punched her arm. Then I realized something, "Ohmygosh, Juniper! I haven't had any visions since you changed. Maybe I only get them about humans...."

"Maybe. Hey, have you been crying?" she asked. She reached her hand out to wipe my face.

I nodded.

"Liv...what is it? You have this really hot guy here who I saw you kissing, which I want details about by the way. Life can't that so bad."

"J...I...your body landed in my lap after Aiden slit your throat. Even though you're here now, it's an image I doubt I'll ever forget." Tears started falling again at the memories. Juniper reached to hug me, her eyes welling up, too.

"I'm so sorry I....I didn't really believe you, Liv. I'm so sorry."

"It's ok. You're here now. That's all that matters," I said with a smile.

We hugged a bit longer. "Juniper...what are you going to tell your parents?" I asked.

She wasn't really paying attention to me, though. Her face concentrated on Mark across the room. He and Scott were picking up chairs and some of the mess we had made. It seemed that both men wanted to get their ladies far from here.

"Go," I urged her as I hugged her chilled body. She didn't have the coldness of death, but she didn't have the warmth that I did either. "We'll talk later."

"I love you, Liv. I'll call you tomorrow," she said with a squeeze and bounced toward Mark, only she was sidetracked by Anna.

Sadie walked up beside me, smiling as she said, "So...you gonna call him Scott or Mr. Sexy?"

I laughed and said, "Both. Scott is sexy. I know he's your brother...but...Look. At. Him."

She pushed me while laughing and said, "Shut up. Eww. Gross. Now I won't be able to sleep tonight."

"Thank you. For everything, Sadie. You've helped me so much..." I said, hugging her hard.

She hugged back, saying, "Anytime. I have a feeling you're going to be my sister soon," her face held a wide grin. I avoided the comment, because I was only seventeen after all. A thought occurred to me, and I decided to ask her about something. "Aiden hasn't been to my house because of the wards you put up, right? That's why he always stops on the street and texts..."

She nodded, still grinning. I would be proud, too, if I were a young sorceress who had held off one of the most powerful beings in her world.

"Good job," I said and patted her on the arm.

"Olivia." I turned when I heard Anna call my name, realizing she was still here. I bade Sadie goodbye, promising

I'd see her later, and walked over to where Anna was standing near the door.

"Miss Anna, who knew you were more than you seemed?" I said. I reached out to give her a big hug. Juniper was at her other side, looking suspiciously sneaky.

"Of course, my darling. Things are never as they seem," she said with a radiant smile.

"I'll have to remember that," I said with an awkward giggle. My eyes darted back and forth between her and Juniper, but I couldn't figure out what mischief they were up to.

"Liv, Miss Anna was just telling me about how much Scott talks about you. He's really in love with you, but why didn't you tell me he was visiting you in your dreams?" she questioned.

My eyes widened, and I looked from Anna to Juniper and back, "Uh...you know about that Miss Anna?" I asked nervously.

"Don't worry, my dear. I don't know what happened. Though from your reddened cheeks, I'd guess it is best I don't know." She laughed and pulled me in for a hug, "You are destined to do magnificent things, Olivia, and you are destined to be with my grandson. And to think, you didn't want to meet him."

Shocked, I just stared at her. She had tried to set me up, and I hadn't been interested. "Oh, yeah, I forgot about that...um...I'd love to meet him, Miss Anna, but see I already have..."

Anna laughed and Juniper punched my arm with a slight look of hurt on her face. "You didn't tell me that you were meeting a really hot guy in your dreams?"

I shrugged. "I didn't think you'd believe me. I had a hard time believing it myself."

"Still. You should have told me," she pouted playfully.

Punching her arm, I asked, "Why aren't you with Mark? You left me for him like five minutes ago!"

"Cauuuse," she said. "I forgot I needed to thank Ms. Anna for saving my life and stuff," she shrugged. She may be immortal, but she was still the same old Juniper.

Chuckling, I said, "And stuff."

I shook my head at them, and we collapsed into a three way hug. Never would I have imagined my best friend would die, I would meet my true love, and find out the dress maker I'd been going to for years was a powerful sorceress all on the same night. I wouldn't have believed it if I didn't have the blood soaked gown and powers to prove it. I looked around at our little group. We were all giggling as we tried to get up. That's when I heard Scott's deep voice calling for me.

SCOTT

I checked the room to make sure Mark and I had gotten everything cleaned up. Sadie helped us some, but the other three ladies had been busy giggling and acting like girls, so she left to join. I hated to interrupt, but it was time for Livvie and me to finally get some alone time. We had a lot of talking to do. Jogging over to the spot where they fell into a heap, I looked around at them as the giggles got louder. "Are you ladies all right?" I asked. A grin played at my cheeks.

Livvie's eyes shone and she said, "Yes, Scott, we're fine."

My heart jumped every time she said my name. I helped them all up, leaving Livvie for last. I wanted to hold her and never let go. I gave her a knowing look, and her eyes widened in surprise and excitement. Her luscious lips spread into a wide grin, and I couldn't take my eyes off of them. I had already told Mark and Sadie goodbye. I grabbed my grandma for a hug and told her I'd see her tomorrow. She looked like she was trying to bite her tongue about something, but I couldn't worry about that now. All that was on my mind was Livvie.

I held her close as I guided her to my truck. It wasn't the newest model, but it was my baby. After getting her settled in the passenger's seat, I slipped in the driver's and looked at her nervously twirling her thumbs. "Livvie? Is there something wrong?" I asked, worry clutching my heart.

"Um...I'm just...you know our dreams? How you would visit me?"

"Yes..."

"Well...I'm not really that experienced! I'm nervous about what's going to happen," she exclaimed, her rosy cheeks turning bright red.

I stifled a laugh and reached for her hand. I squeezed it and said, "Hey, no worries. I'm not expecting anything tonight, or ever. I just want to spend time with you."

She smiled and her shoulders relaxed, "Ooook."

She didn't seem to be completely calm, though. I saw her out of the corner of my eye as I drove, clutching her hands until her knuckles turned white. I reached over and grasped her hand. The softness of her skin melted in mine. She sighed as my thumb caressed her palm. I didn't want her to worry about whether or not we would act out our dreamwalking. Sex was close to the last thing on my mind. I wanted her to feel safe and get her cleaned up. Besides, after all of the power usage, I needed to eat to energize myself. Since she was new to her powers, she would need restoring, too.

We drove down the deserted road. At 1 a.m., I wouldn't expect there to be many people out in this town. Livvie sat reclined in the seat, though she seemed a million miles away. I couldn't help but worry.

A lot had happened, and I wouldn't blame her a bit if she was overwhelmed. She found out her wannabe date was an ancient, evil sorcerer. As if that wasn't enough, she also found out she had powers no one could explain, and she watched her best friend die and be brought back to life. I was surprised she wasn't crying in a corner somewhere all night, but no, not my Livvie. She was being strong and taking things as they came. I admired her strength.

I turned onto my street. The houses were all multiple stories, taller than they were wide with large, well-kept yards. My parents' home was older, like something out of a movie. It was a huge white house with green shutters and a screened in wrap-around porch. The shutters were precisely the shade of green as our family's sorcerer color. Of course, there were flowers adorning the front yard as well as a few garden statues. The garage held two cars, and my apartment was located above it. I pulled into it and released her hand.

I turned to Livvie, looking for her reaction. Her eyes were wide and she looked amazed. Even with a blood splattered dress and black matted hair, she was the most beautiful girl I'd ever laid eyes on. She looked surprised when I jumped out and ran around to open her door, and she lifted her delicate hand to mine. I led her to the stairs and told her about my living situation.

"This is my apartment up here. It's small, just a bedroom, bath, and a kitchen/living area. I do most of my dining and hanging out in my parents' house anyway, so it works out for me." I opened the door and placed my hand on the small of her back, nudging her in first.

"Oh, wow...I really like it, Scott. And this...this is the place where we met in some of my dreams." She turned to me.

"Yes it is," I agreed with a smile.

She looked around, taking it all in. The mirror on the wall showed her reflection, earning a horrified reaction. However, I thought she looked as gorgeous as ever.

"I'm awful! I can't believe this night turned out this way. I must be a dreadful sight for you," she cried out. She truly seemed devastated by her appearance.

"Livvie...you're gorgeous to me as you are, but I understand your feelings. Would you like to take a shower? I can find something for you to put on."

"Oh, yes, please!" she exclaimed, her eyes growing bright with excitement.

"It's right through that door." I pointed to my left, "There are towels on the shelf, and I'll send some clothes in."

"Send clothes in...? What...How?"

Her head cocked to the side in confusion.

"I'm a sorcerer, remember?"

"Oh, yeah." She giggled and turned to the bathroom.

Her hips moved in a tantalizing way, and my mind drifted. The fear of losing her was gone, and my mind was full of kissing, loving, and holding her. Just having her here with me in the flesh was amazing. I rid my mind of the thoughts as I rummaged through my clothing. Livvie was tiny, so anything I had was going to be too big, but she couldn't walk around in a blood and ooze splattered dress. Finally, I found an old pair of sweats from when I was younger, and a smaller shirt for a tighter fit. Hopefully these would work.

I supposed I could conjure her some clothing, but there was something intriguing about the thought of her wearing mine. It seemed sexy. So I stuck with that.

OLIVIA

The hot shower did wonders for my exhaustion. The night had been awful. I was still a little shell shocked. So much happened, and Aiden still wanting me was heavy on my mind. But I didn't want to think about that now. I was in Scott's apartment, and I would not let anything ruin that for me.

I put on the sweats and tank top he sent in. They were both a few sizes too big. I had no bra with me because I couldn't wear one with the dress. Oh, well, I suppose this was better than being covered in Juniper's blood and Aiden's...well, goo. My hair was wet, giving it a wild look. If Scott really loved me...well, this would be the test. If he could find me attractive now, he was definitely a keeper.

I took one last, quick glance in the mirror and stepped out of the bathroom. I looked in the bedroom, my stomach tightening with nervousness. Scott wasn't there. I walked to the living area and saw he was in the kitchen. He'd changed into jeans and another buttoned shirt with the sleeves rolled up to his elbows. His dark hair was messy, and he looked amazing. My breath caught in my throat, and I could barely move. I wanted him so badly. I knew I loved him. Just being around him had proven it to me. My heart fluttered as I stepped toward him. "Hey. I'm all clean now," I said with a timid smile.

His eyes took me in, a hunger in them that I imagined my own had. "You clean up very nicely."

"Oh, come on! I look awful. These are way too big," I said as I pulled the clothes out from me, to emphasize the big.

"You look great," he said and he put his hands around my waist.

I couldn't help but giggle when he said that. I knew I looked far from great. He pulled me closer, his hands under the bottom of my shirt. I gasped. My whole body was raging from the intimate contact. His soft lips took mine, and a moan started deep in my throat. My hands went up to his hair, running through it and tugging at the ends. I wanted him, no, needed him, to be closer to me. Our kissing was intense, with our lips moving in unison and our tongues taking turns exploring the other's mouth. The kissing in the dreams was passionate, but this was out of this world. My head was foggy from kissing, and my body was lit on fire. I pulled way, my hands running down his chest. "Scott."

His eyes were full of desire for me. He looked at me with an intensity I'd never seen before. "Livvie."

"I'm not ready," I said softly, biting my bottom lip.

He pulled me closer, one arm around my waist and the other caressing my head. "I just want to be with you, Livvie. I don't care in what way."

I leaned my face back from his chest, looking up into his deep eyes. "Really?" I asked quietly.

He nodded with a slight smile. The longing was still in his eyes, but the fire had subdued a tiny bit. I squeezed his waist tightly, breathing in his scent. I knew I had to ask the questions burning in my mind, but I didn't know how to get started. "Scott...I...I have questions."

"Ok," he said, smiling and eager.

"Did you ever...when you watched me...was it ever in awkward situations? Like the bathroom or shower or anything?"

"What? Gosh, no, Livvie! That would be an invasion of privacy. I care for you. I wouldn't do that."

Sighing, I could feel the weight of the worry lifting. While I cared for Scott, I had worried about what all he had seen when he watched me.

"Were you really concerned about that, baby?" he asked, his voice low.

I nodded, biting my lip again. He moved away from me. He walked to the living area, slumping in a seat in a defeated way. My heart was breaking, seeing how upset he was. I carefully made my way to him, crouching on my knees in front of him. "Scott, I've fallen in love with you in my dreams, but this is all new to me. I want to know everything. I'm sorry if I upset you." I reached out to his hand, grasping it in mine. He squeezed back, and his other hand played with my hair. I closed my eyes, sighing as his fingers massaged my scalp and relaxed my body. I leaned my head in, almost snuggling his hand, and giggled softly.

"What is it, my love?" he whispered gently.

I lifted my body until I was face to face with him. I leaned in and gave him a soft kiss on his cheek. "I just can't believe I'm really here with you. I really thought I was going crazy there for a while," I said with a laugh.

He leaned his forehead into mine, our eyes level. "You aren't crazy. Well...you may be crazy about me, but that's it," he said with a wink.

I smiled and thought about how true that statement was. I was definitely crazy about him. "I want to know everything about you. I feel like you know so much about me, but I'm still in the dark."

He smiled and said, "Ask me anything."

I scrunched my lips up and put on my best thinking face. "Hmm...let's start with simple. What's your full name?"

"Scott Andrew Tabors. S-A-T. My grandma used to say I was so lazy because my parents gave me S-A-T as initials."

I laughed at that because I could see Anna saying it. "I can't believe Anna is your grandmother. I've been going to her boutique for years."

"If only we'd known..."

"Yeah..." I smiled wistfully. "Ok, what are all your favorites? Color, holiday, animal, anything and everything."

He groaned and thought about the question. "That's loaded. Ok...green, your birthday, horses, food is pancakes and chicken. You know I love art." He paused to think. "I don't know what else you want to know," he said with a magnificent grin.

I climbed up into his lap. The chair was small but perfect for a cozy conversation. I snuggled in closer to his chest and said, "I told you...I want to know everything."

"Everything is so vague. Be specific. We have forever for everything. What do you want to know right this second?"

Forever. And he said my words were loaded. "Do you have any pets? Tell me about your brothers. Are they as awesome as Sadie?"

"No pets. Santos is awesome...Sebastian, however...he's...I'm not sure how to describe him. He doesn't really like family time. He's not close to any of us." Sadness passed over his face, and I felt bad for bringing it up.

"Oh. I'm sorry," I said as my fingers slid over his cheek bones. I traced the outline of his jaw, and he closed his eyes. A soft smile spread on his face, and he sighed happily. "I like your face. It's so strong and masculine, but comforting at the same time."

His eyes opened and peered at me. "You are too much, love. I'm so glad you're here. I have to shower, though."

I nodded and reluctantly got off his lap. I held on to his hand until he slipped away, then I sat in bliss until he returned.

SCOTT

As much as I didn't want to leave Livvie for one minute, I set off for a shower. I needed to wash the stench of the night away from me so I could enjoy my time with my love. The shower revitalized me. My body was achy from the fighting, but the hot water helped. I hurried through it, though, not really enjoying it like I normally would have. My heart was happy to have Livvie here with me, and I wanted to cherish every second after this horrid night.

Livvie and I stayed up half the night talking and getting to know each other. After our difficult conversation about espying and my quick shower, we had curled up on the couch. I started the conversation and told her everything about me; information ranged from my other family members to what color my favorite socks were. She listened intently, her beautiful face studying mine while I spoke.

After that, we moved to the kitchen. At 2:30a.m., we mixed pancakes after we both realized it had been awhile since we'd eaten anything. Making breakfast with her in my kitchen felt natural and right. She told me about her family while we prepared our food, her soft lips detailing and describing every important person in her life. Jealousy coursed through me as I realized they all had such a long history with her, while I only possessed a few sweet moments in her dreams.

Shaking the thoughts, I watched intently as her soft body glided through my kitchen. Her delicate hands whipped the batter while her hair bounced in unison. The pants I gave her were too big and her hip bones kept peeking out, driving me crazy.

"Scott," she asked, her voice pulling me from her hips. She looked at me curiously, a smirk on her lips. "Are you listening? I need a skillet to cook these in."

"Oh, ok. They're right here," I said. I opened the cabinet above her head.

"What were you thinking about?" she asked and poked me in the ribs.

I smiled and shook my head. That, I wasn't going to tell her.

"Scott!" She attacked me, trying her best to tickle me. She soon realized that I wasn't ticklish though, so all of her effort was for nothing.

I held her in a bear hug off the floor, kissing her nose when it was level with my mouth. "I like cooking with you."

She giggled. "I like cooking with you, too. Even if it is after two in the morning."

The White Aura

We finished flipping our pancakes, though we burned a few in the process. After a dual effort on clean-up, we stood awkwardly, realizing it was time to sleep.

"Sco—"

"Liv—"

We both spoke at the same time. Looking at each other, we laughed. I gestured for her to go first.

"Scott, I'd really like to sleep in the room with you tonight. I want you to hold me. I think I would feel safer that way."

My heart was beating faster and faster. I nodded. I was thinking the same thing. "I want you to. I promise I won't try anything."

"I know that," she said as she reached to touch my face. She stared into my eyes intensely, the green glowing with desire. "I just don't want it to be too tempting for either of us, that's all. If it is, I can sleep somewhere else."

"No," I said firmly, "you are not sleeping somewhere else. I need you with me so I can know you're safe."

She looked worried and kept biting her lip. She was nervous, and I got the feeling there was more on her mind.

"What is it?" I asked quietly.

"When will Aiden come back for me?" she asked in a deathly whisper.

I pulled her closer. "I don't know, love. But know that nothing will happen to you. I'll protect you."

She glanced up with a smirk on her face. "You're going to protect me?" she asked.

I laughed. She made a point. She did pretty well for herself tonight once she had tapped into her powers. "Ok, let me rephrase. I want to protect you, but I know you can protect yourself. Is that better?" I asked as I kissed her forehead.

"Yes. Thank you," she said with a laugh. She squinted and turned her head to the side, like she had just realized something.

"What is it now?"

"Do you know what other powers I may have?" she asked, pulling away from me a little. She stared down at her hands, inspecting them with a great intensity. She looked up at me, a little mesmerized. "I shot fire out of my hands, and it didn't burn me. Why?"

"Because it was coming from you. It won't burn you if you create it."

"And the visions...they only work on humans?"

I shrugged. "I don't have that power, so I'm not sure. It seems that way, though."

"I didn't get one when I touched either of my parents ..." she thought aloud. "I wonder what else I can do?" she asked quietly.

I locked my forehead with hers. I looked into her eyes and saw the burning desire to know about herself. "We'll figure it out, all right? We do have suspicions that you're a mix of beings...meaning your parents are from the paranormal world, Livvie."

She nodded, her face conveying panic she didn't voice. I reached my hand out to her, palm up, so she could put hers in it. Locking fingers we walked down the hall to the bedroom. I fluffed the pillows and got an extra one from the closet. I knew from our dreams that she liked to sleep on two pillows.

"So which side do you sleep on?" she asked.

"I usually sleep in the middle," I said with a laugh, "but I'll take the left. I know you like the right."

She smiled and crawled in on her side. She looked small in my king sized bed. Her red hair seemed to darken against the whiteness of my pillows. I turned off the light and crossed back to the bed. When I slipped in, I could hear her breathing quicken. I lay facing her. I reached out to hold her in my arms. She slid her body over and rested her head in the crook of my arm. Her hand caressed my chest and a flutter went through my heart. I inhaled sharply, and she took the hint, moving her hand back.

I touched her face, and she lifted her head onto my shoulder. I wrapped my arms around her in a big hug.

She giggled and pulled away. "I like this," she sighed.

"Me too."

Her eyes were drooping as she looked at me, a soft smile crossing her face every so often.

"You look exhausted, my darling. Perhaps you should rest," I said. I kissed her forehead.

"I know. I probably should. I called my parents and left a message saying I was with Juniper. Isn't that awful?"

"Nah. We're going to them tomorrow. We need answers about what exactly you are and where your powers come from. We can tell them the truth then."

She sighed and nodded. Her eyes looked heavy, like she would pass out soon. "Mr. Sexy," she whispered.

"Yes, Livvie."

"I...I want to say that I'm so happy we met. I'm so glad you saw me that day outside of the coffee shop."

My heart was full of love for this amazing woman in my bed. I caressed her hair and said, "My Livvie, we were destined to be together. I'm so happy I found you."

We kissed again, a gentl soft, kiss full of love and promise for our future. I was happy, but something was nagging at me. I couldn't quite figure out what. She had drifted off to sleep when it hit me. The realization of the most important thing I could have forgotten. My stomach clenched and I gasped for breath as it washed over me. We had met before the curse allowed. In all of the confusion and drama of the night, it had somehow escaped my mind. Livvie was going to die.

Want to keep up to date on new releases? Sign up for my newsletter! http://eepurl.com/DkPmr

Book two, The Vessel, now available! Get it wherever ebooks and paperbacks are sold.

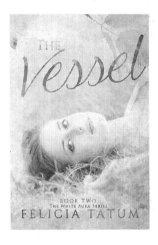

About the Author

The White Aura is my debut novel. I live in Tennessee with my daughter and kitty. Since the age of twelve, writing has been my passion and I'm so excited to finally be sharing it with the world. I love to connect with readers, so please get in touch!

www.feliciatatum.com

www.facebook.com/feliciatatumwriter

www.twitter.com/authorfelicia

Acknowledgments

First, I would like to thank my mom for all her support during the writing of this novel. She believed in me when I didn't believe in myself and I'm so thankful for that. All of the authors out there who motivated, encouraged, and supported me...it means the world to me and I hope I can be half as helpful to all of you! And finally, my friends who have been excited and supportive during my craziness. I love you all!

50674776R00139

Made in the USA
Lexington, KY
24 March 2016